WHAT BOOKS PRESS

AN IMPRINT OF

THE GLASS TABLE

COLLECTIVE

LOS ANGELES

ROMANCE WORLD

ROMANCE WORLD

TAMAR PERLA CANTWELL

Library of Congress Cataloging-in-Publication Data

Names: Cantwell, Tamar Perla, 1965- author.
Title: Romance world : stories / Tamar Perla Cantwell.
Other titles: Romance world (Compilation)
Description: Los Angeles : What Books Press, an imprint of The Glass Table
    Collective, 2023. | Summary: "These stories present textured characters
    who, with clear-eyed awareness, seek to build relationships and shape
    better lives from fragments of yearning and self-love"-- Provided by
    publisher.
Identifiers: LCCN 2023024884 | ISBN 9798986625874 (paperback)
Subjects: LCGFT: Short stories.
Classification: LCC PS3603.A636 R66 2023 | DDC 813/.6--dc23/eng/20230608
LC record available at https://lccn.loc.gov/2023024884

Cover art: Gronk, *Untitled*, media, 2022
Book design by ash good, www.ashgood.com

What Books Press
363 South Topanga Canyon Boulevard
Topanga, CA 90290

WHATBOOKSPRESS.COM

For my family: Shira and John, Raymond, and Arielle

CONTENTS

BABYLOVE

HER EX CALLS again about their only daughter, the one they did not have.

"How's my baby girl?" he asks.

"Who?" Annie says, startled out of her reality show. "What?"

"I hope she's feeling better," he says.

He wants to know if the toys arrived: seven colors in a paint box, a baton with white leatherette ends wrapped in purple cellophane, an old-fashioned straw doll in a gingham dress.

"She's too young for the baton," Annie says, "and the dolly looks straight out of *Children of the Corn*."

"She requested those specifically."

"You know—" Annie says. Then, more kindly, "But please, I mean, stop it. Please."

She turns off the television and goes to bed, dreams of overcrowded beaches, her toddler who needs to be changed, filthy restrooms. Locks that wriggle free. A house with a stove and a pan on fire; rain that falls in sheets between plexiglass walls. Annie finds her, at last: a cartoon girl sleeping in a mausoleum drawer. The drawer is fur-lined, the girl cozy but unsmiling.

A few months and he calls again, urgent: "I have some information."

Gently, Annie says, "She sees us here, together and talking, and she's happy. She understands, Paul."

"Just trying to deliver a message," he mutters.

This time Annie feels the baby's presence. "You can go, now," Annie says into the empty room. "I've got it covered." The baby shrinks slightly, hesitates. "You've got no body," Annie calls out, "I have the body here!" She is livid, but the baby is leaving, leaves, will stay gone for a while, maybe.

On the doctor's table Annie barely feels the effects of the Valium. She squeezes the nurse's offered hand and wills herself out of her body, her pain, for the few minutes it takes to perform the procedure. She imagines she sees the baby girl, curled on her side and perfect in a pool that could be beet juice, aspic: the baby is a pretty jelly in a small silver bowl. Of course Annie never sees her, never knows if she is a daughter. The baby hangs on, regardless, the most powerful thing Annie has had to destroy, up to this point.

They decide to put it behind them and go to Hawaii like they could do this as easily as changing tables, asking for a better view. Stepping from the plane into the oppressive overcast of the Big Island is the seventh sign of how desperate things have gotten between them. The plane ride itself is the sixth, so different from their first time, Paul's bonus from the firm, when they were excited to be alone together and everything was a treat from the cheap champagne to the miniature hot fudge sundaes. Now seated next to a family of missionaries, they are so high on crystal that nothing is certain but Paul's irritation with the woman whose shoe is tap-tapping at the back of his seat throughout the flight. Then stepping off, Paul is sure he left his cell phone on the plane and not at the apartment or in the car, and he goes back for it or they leave it, paranoid about re-entering security—Annie can't say what really happens. Just that their descent into hell has begun.

Their room in the lux, beachfront hotel is dazzling with a private lanai and a big, soft bed, but they can't see it. They're getting high. This is difficult to look back on since Annie knows it turns out badly. At the time, all they wanted was to see. High, Annie could walk down a busy sidewalk, and instead of her usual habit, self-consciously training her eyes away from people, she could look into each face and make the connection, recognize them as kin. She could hear their private conversations as if she suddenly had wolf ears: "Have you noticed how many beautiful girls are out today?" She could become one of those girls, seeing her beauty though their eyes.

Their daughter never grows up to be beautiful. She grows into something—Annie knows it makes no sense, she doesn't believe in such things, but the baby is a winged chunkalunk, a drooling, purring demon. In a tower, the baby braids her baby-fine hair into a weak, blond rope, lets it fall to the Earth, climbs down to find them. Here they are! Sucking down smoke, rolling around like wrestlers, yelling, biting, pummeling. They throw bowls of water at each other, scream, "Die, witch, die!" They rip books apart, and jewelry, and Annie pounds Paul's back as if she could beat the poison out of him. They are like frenzied gods who tear the heads from their sacrifices and drink the blood. The baby looks on adoringly, thumb in her mouth, gurgling at every hurled object and word. She has no choice in this; she loves them simply and beyond reason.

In Hawaii, the old alchemy fails to work. Gold turns to lead in their lungs and in their hands. The amount of money they spend— charged to cards they will not be able to pay off for years—buys them no pleasure. Annie gets her own room, finally, because she can't stand the fighting. There is no love, just a rock that takes away the fear before replacing it with an entire world turned against them; there is no love, just exorcism after exorcism, and still the world hates. The beach sand glitters with garnet, feldspar, quartz: they would smoke it if they could. Everything tastes bitter, and she can't imagine why they have come here to crash and burn, why they insist upon the rhythm of regret, why they must climb again to the top of the volcano and jump inside.

It is a while since they have seen each other, and they meet at the movies. In the late afternoon light, she observes Paul as a stranger, too-thin and nervous, already worn by his twenty-something years. They buy pizza, but he doesn't eat his. They watch *Dr. Doolittle*, and Paul is seeing the sub-text, the hidden messages, the way the women in the theater look at him condemningly—he is wearing an amulet for protection and the mark of havoc on his forehead, in his creased and troubled brow. Sitting between them and settled in now, the baby is gumming popcorn into butter-flavored pabulum. Annie wears her tight and sparkly *bad kitty* t-shirt, but it doesn't make her feel sexy, just as if she's advertising. They are only three ghosts, so release them, Annie thinks. Dear Dr. Doolittle, she prays to the make-believe world, to Eddie Murphy, please make the voices stop. Make Paul better. Make me better. Make the sickness go away.

"Bad mommy," the baby says, sucking Pepsi out of her bottle. She giggles at the talking animals on the big screen, presses first into Annie's side, hiding her face against Annie's breast, then flops her golden head across Paul's twitching thighs. In the baby's heaven, they are always together like this, the three of them holding hands in a sea of luminosity, a family of lighthouses blinking love signals at one another.

When the phone rings, Annie is not so surprised to hear his voice. A year has passed, and he is on the East Coast at a mountain festival, seeing colors. Thousands of miles from the firm, his old connections, he says, "I feel good! Strong. Sold the Lexus and bought a bicycle." Unasked, he describes his companions who sound like hobbits and elves, wear women's cast-off clothing, walk on stilts.

"Did you get my present?" his voice pitches and wheels, exuding bells and wildflowers. He tells her he knows when the cops are about to pull up beside him, recognizes the treefolk and animal spirits, cultivates medicinal herbs and grasses, will soon master the craft of transmutation. She thinks, with a relief so great it hurts to admit it, she may not need to see him again.

A week later, the package arrives. It has been lost in the mail, and she wonders where it went, who handled and dented it, sprinkled it with fairy dust or baser vibrations. It is filled with seashells. These are encased in a paper globe, like an ornament, and are evidence of what Paul and Annie have made together, their beautiful, broken plans. They are mixed with grits of sand, and they rattle when she shakes them out onto the kitchen table: mottled Venus, periwinkle, baby bonnet, slipper, razor, cask, angel wings. At first she doesn't see the gold band, two times too big for her own finger, how she had to guess his size. Annie feels something inside her begin to claw to the surface, shuts it down hard before it has time to flower and bleed.

On their first, first-class flight together after Paul's firm loses a big case but still bills millions, the ordinary ice cream they are offered tastes exciting and foreign so far from the surface of the planet. Then they join the mile-high club—the digital age, they joke later—beneath their first-class blanket. Buzzing with sugar and sex, they circle over Maui and don't notice how their shoes tap the seats in front of them. As the wheels of the plane scrape the hot asphalt, Paul does not yet say, "I want you to have my baby, baby," and Annie does not yet say, "Let's get married first, my love."

But seconds after they enter their deluxe hotel room with a penthouse view of the Pacific Ocean bordered by three silvery blue, interconnected swimming pools, Annie pulls her dress over her head the way she has seen it done in movies, and Paul reaches for her, helps her onto his lap so that they make the kind of fit she has read about. She rocks over him in a mindless delirium, high on the proof of his success that will surely continue, his eyes that remain open, locked on hers even as she goes blind with pleasure. Then there is nothing else they can think of to do but order delicious, expensive food and cocktails and stare out into the circling sea.

TRIAGE

I AM NOT sure when I decide to break with convention, to put my tenure at risk, but it is sometime between receiving the "bomb with love" text from Tallulah and reading the student essay that misspells "surfer" as "suffer" and uses "motherfucking" as a verb.

"I really want to love them," I say to her.

"If you're speaking euphemistically, it's a bad idea. You'll wobble through Monday morning lectures, and eventually the deans will know you're up to no good."

"But how else to yank them out of their stupors—the boys, I mean. The girls seem to wake up on their own."

"If you're trying to get back at the philanderer writers like Updike, and—well, Updike, it's a bad idea. Have you even read anything besides *Couples?*"

My silence is an admission of guilt.

She sighs, humoring me. "You must keep a notebook, then, for each," she says, "and turn it into a Project."

We act as if we are talking reasonably for two youngish professors at a small, ivy-wreathed college in a town that is rarely in the news. I am about to start loving my students—yes, euphemistically.

Tallulah sends me a photo of Iranian nurses holding rifles. She has marked a face with yellow and written, *Could be your twin!* Maybe she believes these images will pull me out of myself and back to my classroom. But once there, while giving my students pieces of what I believe to be true, I search faces and find this one, haloed in yellow highlighter. We will sleep together, and I will lean into something like love. I have tried loving them objectively and failed, so now I am attempting this new thing. With this method, I won't cry in frustration when they don't understand what I'm trying to tell them. My not understanding them will become their greatest allure.

It is Monday and these last five minutes have been about culverts, of all things, because Springfield wants to know, "What's a culvert?" and I want to give Springfield whatever he wants. This Faulkner we are reading, I profess to understanding, and when I say something unsafe, un-professorial, their lashes lift, for a moment, with light; their eyes stop gnawing at their phones, and I almost can't stand how easy they are to manipulate. My necklace itches, my fingertips burn, my watch jimmies loose from my wrist and flies across the room.

Sometimes I open the top button of my blouse when they stop chewing things obsessively, rest my chin in my hands, lower my voice to softness. Springfield doesn't say much when we're alone, so I relish his public voice. In front of his classmates, he's good at getting specific; why won't he do this in his essays?

"Culverts: a good question, Springfield." I ask for a lot, make them listen to endless talk of rebar caging, dozens of rocks down the shaft if not, all the while metal siphons carrying water away from shallow, wooden runoffs shaped into a vee, the way part of me is shaped. Finally, it is just a drain beneath a road. Finally, there is nothing malign or devious, nothing that hurts too badly, just snowmelt. I stick to them like Velcro and take it seriously, the responsibility. Here in this room, I mean to say, my private room, there are no crappy motions, no tiresome air shows, no fast-food fictions. What is attached will be released gently, with some degree of care.

Since I started my revenge against Updike, there have been several of these, but lately I am for Springfield. They have become my best muses and excuses, unexpected perks. It is late in the afternoon when Springfield asks me, "Why do we have to read Faulkner?"

"Because it's a big world, and we need to know how to live in it," I say, borrowing from Tallulah's repertoire of aphorisms.

"I think you're nicer than they say," he says, eyes closed. "You have nice brown eyes."

"Except they're blue," I say.

"That's what I said," Springfield says. "Your eyes are the bluest. Do you wear contacts?"

Springfield is this month's purpose, its reward, the next best thing to a sabbatical. Apologies to Springfield, for I am stockpiling his charm, his murmur, the way he saves me from another rote day I would have turned my back on. He is my martyr for a while, my satyr-saint combination plate. He gives me all the pleasure I would not give myself, just by being Springfield.

Now that I am several seasons into the Project, when these boys no longer require my immediate care, I might just die, I decide. Or retire. Having given up on acquiring stuff, somewhat—I pay the mortgage on a tiny house with a renovated bathroom and still drive a battle-scarred Jeep—I indulge in this other avarice. My emotional age matches their chronological one, I explain in defense. Gloatingly, I tell my friend that my writing is progressing, fifty pages deep. She tallies on her fingers, names the names she knows. Whistles.

"Not bad. Are you prioritizing them by GPA or by credit hours?" she asks.

I tell her that I will piece it together later. Right now, I'm working on Springfield.

She laughs out her nose, but can't resist, in turning: "Maybe this will be the book!"

Her own, *Prenuptial Idyll, from Barn to Castle,* has been optioned. Last semester her work-to-leisure suit was St. John; now it's Chanel.

When Springfield pulls off my skirt, pulls it down over my hips and runs his hands up to my throat, investigating everything along the way, he says, "You are so...solid." Although this is not entirely true, I smile to be so something for him, especially this thing. Ambivalent, I have touched older devotees gone soft with grief, with disappointment, the resigned skin parting from muscle, have accepted their premature resignations. So I am pleased to offer this mirage. I watch him press his fingers into my arm, my belly; did I say he isn't talkative, I meant he talks simply—his poetry is blunt and medieval, like thrown fruit.

"Springfield," I say, "You are just the right size for me," and he likes this, lifts me into the air, settles me around his waist, lets me relax against him like a child. When he puts me down, there is no change in his breathing. I can find nothing wrong with Springfield. Even his chipped front tooth is irresistible.

A classroom is a difficult room to teach in. A classroom implies leveling before raising; we're bricklayers without a master builder after lunch break, our tongues scalded and thick from thermos soup. If someone falls off the scaffolding, the students want to call it a day. But this one could be a miracle, could come out of it walking, could walk out of it laughing, shining a different sort of light.

I bring the word *love* into my classroom. I make them read *Madame Bovary, my* classroom, and I do all the talking. They would skip Mrs. B. altogether, but I want them to ask why she dies hard, why hers is a life worth examining. One girl tries valiantly, her effort as conspicuous as the monogram on her cashmere cardigan, and we find our way around words of relationship and property, a mention of Brontë, but it's always the details that get them down. They would kill Emma sooner to escape her, to get back to their own dramas. Just like her, they fear the deadening quality of their routines, and novels like this are too much work, too little distraction.

Afterward I stomp around with a chocolate chip scone, so over the expensive, dry pastry and certain students—the emotionally barricaded

back-row sprawler with a shaved head and stepdad issues, the pen
tapper who also pops his jaw obsessively, the effusive boy who rolls his
eyes and hovers over occupied desks even after lecture has started. I hate
myself for fighting them, but they pit their facts against my fictions,
and I always come up wanting. I toss the scone in the trash and
consider that my self-loathing is another reason for wanting Springfield
so stubbornly, the others before him.

It is absurd, what I'm wanting from Springfield. In bed, my bed,
I'm falling over him like a lukewarm shower; I'm bringing words of love
into the room then trying to shake them off.

"Springfield," I say, "Whenever I talk about us and use the word
love, you must insert the word *having* afterward, and know that what I
really mean exists somewhere between the two."

He looks at me through half-opened lids and says nothing. I don't
want to keep him forever. I don't want him to lock out his roommate
so we can use their room for an hour. I don't want to lie together on
the sagging sofa bed, mattress coils abrading our backs and the moist
eyes of used condoms, not all ours, squinting from behind pizza that
has been congealing for days. I don't want to announce through stale,
bong-infused air, "Springfield, I'm going now." Yet I do.

I know what I want him for, and this can last only as long as
class. He is generous and knows this and does his best, comes to me
all appreciation and sometimes startled joy. He tells me, sweetly,
that *I* will be okay; he says this like he knows how everything in the
world works.

In earnest-professor mode I ask myself, "What am I teaching
Springfield?" Then I am distracted by his mint condition, the moment
that hums in him, and I try to imagine his thoughts: from sleek cars
to buoyantly cleavaged girls, to the bloody rigors of asphalt hockey, to
purgatory v. limbo. I don't want to think about him, really. I just want
to feel how good he feels.

"You seem distracted," he says, inside the moment.

"I love—having—you," I say.

Before Springfield there was JayCee, who liked to go to Vegas. He was tall and awkward and kind with two older brothers who had "paid their debt to society." An accident he would not discuss had skewed his face with a vertical scar from cheek to eyebrow. He was famous among instructors for his JayCeeisms—"escape goat" and "foie de vivre" were often repeated—and he insisted on wording his thesis statements as questions. In class he participated strictly for laughs: "I am down with Mr. B., but he is blind to the fact that his freak wants variety as any fine woodchuck would." He was half my age and "reconditioning"—his term—since his last college, where instead of studying he grew abs and pecs and quads like some grow corn, beets and squash.

With JayCee at least, I had no illusions. That is, after much contemplation, I thought in my head that I was sure I knew what I was doing. Now, dear students, which of these sentences is correct?

It is a Thursday, late in the term, and Springfield wants to know why he didn't get an A on an obviously recycled essay. I want to know how we keep going, right through each stock market swindle, presidential rumpus, drought/epidemic/earthquake, invasion, canceled apocalypse.

"You don't have to love them all by yourself," Tallulah coos, passing me in the unhallowed halls. "Perhaps I could help you. Your Benton Springfield—isn't he missing his Misty Isle requirement? Besides, you don't like to keep them past a semester, do you?"

I decide to go to the midnight movie where I don't know what's playing until I get in line. It's the second adaptation of *Lolita*, and I wonder if any of my boys will show, but the clutch is mostly patched corduroy elbows, undyed hair, sensible shoes.

Between handfuls of popcorn and Hot Tamales, I throb, at first, for Jeremy Irons and his piranha teeth, but soon I have to force myself to stay in my seat. "Maybe you'll learn something?" JayCee's voice echoes in my ear, and I suppose I might, something about the kind of wanting that turns people into dust. I don't remember the novel taking this stance, exactly. The film I watch isn't about grabbing at wrong things but instead about how the grabbing itself goes wrong.

Near the end, someone in the back row starts laughing. Heads swivel, curious about the shameless perp in the shadows, but soon we understand that this is a woman who is sobbing uncontrollably. Even more than when little Lo writhed before us on nude Humbert's lap, we voyeurs stew in our discomfort. We pull on our coats as the credits roll and slink out the side door, scrupulously avoiding eye contact.

Although now it is truly late, I walk through eucalyptus and step onto the porch of Hansom House, wait behind one of the Greek columns. I am not really surprised to see Springfield emerge, a girl beside him; they reach for bags of food from a delivery guy. She is a pretty girl and blond and barefoot, and when Springfield reaches out to playfully grab at her exposed, pale stomach, I see that her jeans are unbuttoned, two buttons. I sit down next to the column and wait until the moon is fully visible, until I have enough light to see clearly as I untuck my sweater, my blouse. I place my hand upon the warm skin underneath, sad it is my hand.

It will be Christmas, and I could see him over the break. I lie and say I won't be around; I don't know where I'll be.

"It's all Gucci," Springfield says. I don't understand what he means.

We're in our last days, and the weather is good. I keep repeating this like I'm looking for something I've lost: "Isn't the weather good?" and whoever happens to be there glances past me, up at the sky, and says, "It certainly is!"

Back in my office, when I start giving the same C+ to every paper in the stack, I tell myself to put the pen down. But my hand is insistent, absentmindedly doodling little tic-tac-toe boards in the margins, exes and ohs. I apply thin ribbons of Wite-Out tape, stuff the papers in a drawer and sit dazedly, staring at my own framed, bleary-eyed reflection in the glass of my degrees when the door opens and next semester walks in.

"Whasup," says the mighty Roland Manning, so many first-years named like characters in novels they won't read.

When Roland unbuttons my blouse, he acts with restraint, his choreographed fingers and lips moving in slow-mo. Confusingly, there is always a breeze lifting the dark curls of his pomaded hair. I find myself ripping off his clothes so we can get this skirmish started, professor against student, the hegemony of experience and conviction over ignorance and lassitude. But I already know what will happen next. He will start to talk crit until I want to scream. I interrupt to get us something strong and his a double so he is soon overcome, passed out.

In sleep, I recognize he is nowhere near grown-up, that his job for a while is oblivious youth, to walk in front of my moving car with his earbuds in and his eyes closed in baroque-pop-triphop-arena-rock ecstasy, and if I weren't his teacher, I'd be at a Hotcake Hut at one in the morning, serving him and his drunk, laughing friends bacon with extra grease and then getting up at five a.m. to work on my unpublished manuscript, no harm done.

Roland wants to know if he really needs to buy all the required books. But also, he has heard things about me, that we take class off-campus if the subject dictates and the weather permits, etc. Yes, yes, Mr. Manning, I will see you after the break; I have other matters to tend to right now.

I take my time walking to class where the students are gathered in cliques, hyped up, giggling and flirting. I run through roll and raise my eyes in some pain. All those windows, that cloudless, blue sky, that blinding fall light.

Springfield's hand is up, and I say, "Yes, Springfield?"

"It says here," he says, apropos of nothing, face lit by the glow from his computer tablet, "that during World War II, pancake syrup was called *machine oil*, Jell-O was called *shivering Liz*, and—wait for it—" clear brown eyes skimming the screen, "a paralyzed person was a *stiffy!*" He offers the words with pride as if they make him smarter just in the saying. A few students laugh obligingly, and he is so earnest, so unaware of his shortcomings, that I have to smile. I still want Springfield to have whatever he wants.

What would the old men—Faulkner, Flaubert, and Nabokov—God, and Updike too—say to my students? What were they saying still, through their fictions—that they had been there, done that, roiled with hormones, with great and terrible ideas, fought in pointless wars, lied to themselves, trembled before beauty, thought they would live forever? What do my students hear, and how relevant now are my monologues to their busy lives, their excruciating moments, the endless stretches of time when they are held hostage by adults who won't let them text one another? I tried, Springfield, I want to say. I'm your teacher, and I have something to give you, only it's not what you think it is.

Next week, after finals, I'll tell Springfield that I'll miss him, and I'll mean it. For now, I fidget with my watch, make marks on the board, open a button. This feels like the wrong thing to do, but I turn from the feeling, intent on showing, not telling. The class is silent but breathing as I reach into my bag of tricks and dispense the appropriate remedies—a targeted audience, an emotional appeal, a good, strong thread to tie up loose ends, to stop the bleeding.

ROMANCE WORLD

SANDRA

At Las Olas College, the room reserved for Sandra's presentation is windowless and over-refrigerated. Five rows of recycled plastic chairs with attached, unmovable desklets—you have to be a skinny eighteen-year-old to fit comfortably in these things, she thinks—beg for a real audience. Only four people attend. Two are unfamiliar, revolving-door adjuncts, herself until only recently, she reminds, and the last to arrive is the English Chair. He smiles apologetically and is very tan, and she is glad to see him. Once he is seated, she unveils her Galatea, her obsession since she was a teenager spending summers by the pool, voraciously consuming paperbacks.

Her proposed class, Reading the Romance Novel, will not examine themes in *Jane Eyre* or *Tess of the D'Urbervilles*. She distributes the reading list, and four pairs of eyes squint at *Set Her Free* by Dame Maisy Lightfoote, Barbara Brell's *Three Times Two*, and several titles from the Elegant Heathen series by Cloquet. Sandra ignores a pressing urge to scratch her chest, her belly. The pain of refusing her body's requests is almost unbearable, as is her sudden clarity that women's romantic stories will never pass snuff as a course designation. Nevertheless, she sells.

"Classical yet evolving narrative structures" blah blah "evidenced by the enduring" blah "contemporary Chick Lit's regenerative body." When she has finished, her mouth is dry and her fingers are puffy, sure signs of dehydration. She takes a long drink of water from the plastic bottle she always brings to the classroom, and asks, automatically, "Any questions?" The room practically hisses with exertions to keep mouths shut. There is also an inhale of sexual curiosity. Mercifully, Robert Pratt, Automotive Technology/Mechanical Engineering, wags his hand in the air.

"What would be the incentive for males—for our special lot of service-and-repair primitives, in particular—to enroll? Besides assured proximity to pining females?" He aims his question at the young female adjunct, her lowcut blouse.

"Because these novels are about transformation," Sandra offers, "about being lifted socially, economically, emotionally—"

"But will our Mr. Goodwrenches *desire* to be raised to, made expert in, some kind of Tantra-ahhh experience? Are they not sufficiently challenged by *Émigré Perspectives* and *Women of the Americas?*"

Watching Rob's mouth deliver each word with emphasis and the occasional, fine spray of spit, Sandra recognizes that he has a certain brand of erotic appeal, organic and unrefined, like that dirty looking, but tasty, raw sugar. The spirit of her own ardor for her husband, Marcus, has diminished over seven years, as prophesied, and she's not sure she has the ambition to get it back. Passion simply *takes one over.* She forces herself to focus, to speak.

"What I mean is...who wouldn't want to be raised by love? Emigrant, American, and hormonally distracted college student alike?"

The female adjunct, in sheer paisley tights and a too-short corduroy skirt, coughs into her purse. The male adjunct may have succeeded in falling asleep while keeping his eyes open.

A memory comes to Sandra then, unasked-for, unable to be shaken: her friend from long ago, from elementary school, and their sudden break-apart—she hasn't thought of Angel for years, so why now? Maybe it's the female adjunct, who seems both aware of her body and indifferent to its sexual signaling. Sandra and Angel had done

things together, had constructed elaborate adventures. They had slept
over at each other's houses a hundred times, argued about books, been
there for each other when their families were a mess, before everything
changed. Sandra remembers. She aches to escape into one of her novels.

Then her pitch is over. After all her anxiety, her many evenings and
weekends of preparing and rehearsing, there is no gratifying conclusion.
There never is.

"To be continued…nice work," the Chair smiles warmly, pats
Sandra's shoulder as they exit the icy room and step into sun that
is starting to break through fog. Sandra has always recognized that
the Chair would make an excellent hero in a Lightfoote novel. This
thought, potentially dangerous, cheers her.

It's not quite noon, and she's already pulling into the driveway
of the Rosenblooms, her longtime housesitting gig. Now that she is
tenured, Marcus keeps asking her to give up caretaking the older couple
and their property, but spending time in their sprawl is equivalent to
having a room of her own.

The Rosenblooms have named their acre "The Park in Bloom"
even though to Sandra it seems more like a fire sale that's been dying
to happen since before the first George Bush entered office. Rusted and
rotted deck furniture, termite-breeding "cottages" containing stores
of oily, dirt-caked antiques—barbers' chairs, truck husks and NYC
subway turnstiles—are largely concealed by crop circles of flowering,
head-high thistle, mini-groves of infected citrus trees, and blighted figs.
The Park's floriculture, where it persists, resembles a cottage garden
trampled by elephants.

"We used to keep a *chaniwa*—that's Japanese for tea garden, dear—
until we decided the English style suited us better," Edda has explained
to Sandra, and then, without a wink of humor, "Wouldn't you agree
that our gardeners are artisans?"

The land also boards three large dogs, "Our woodgy-schmoodgy
freedom fighters," who must run wild. Sandra is grateful for the invisible
fence that encircles most of the property and keeps the canine insurgents

out of the neighbors' yards. Through the large picture window in the office in which she works, Sandra often watches the non-English-speaking landscapers clip a few leaves or scoot the dog poop around for no more than a half-hour (admittedly, this feels like a long time—it seems an eternity just to kick a path to the front door) before heading for their trucks and other, more manageable lawns. The Park in Bloom is a daunting grove of humus and hubris, a feral ode to Mother Earth.

Today Sandra is relieved that no lawnmower is interrupting her contemplation. After sorting numerous pages of the Rosenblooms' electronic and snail mail, she closes the blinds, reaches into her soft leather satchel, and retrieves her latest romance from beneath piles of ungraded student papers. It is now early afternoon, after all, siesta time in some sultry Mediterranean city. Curled up in Ed's easy chair (she tries not to think of his narrow, drooping hindquarters occupying the same seat, but such is the curse of the avid reader's imagination—although she loves the lingering odor of his pipe tobacco), she opens her book and begins to read. She goes slowly at first and then voraciously, with greater and greater abandon, letting herself be raised and raised again, razed and ravished by the heady, solitary, extraordinary experience of becoming a character in a story more exciting than her own. She reads until arousal burns through her entire body.

There is a convenient daybed in the office, and she flops onto it like a teenager, flips off her too-tight pumps. Her breath quickens and she reads faster now, but steady, steady, her eyes absorbing each sentence in a measured pace that builds as she loosens her hair clip and lets it fall to the floor. Jezebel, she is a Jezebel of the worst sort! After a while, the book also falls off the side of the bed, relinquished with her contented yawn of dénouement.

She has dozed, but for how long? The light has changed behind the blinds and her skin is damp with unmoving as she peels herself from the cushions. Except for the barking of the dogs, it is quiet outside. She twists her hair up and walks—no, slinks—into the kitchen on bare feet. She replays her short but vivid dream, tries to hold on to its tangible feeling—a meeting on the beach with the English Chair (mildly embarrassing, but she can't *un*dream it), surfboard tucked under his ample bicep, his hair dark with sea water and madly flattering to his squared, sunburned jaw. The narcotic after-effect of the brush with romance is still upon her, and she feels wonderful, entitled to help herself to a beer from the Rosenblooms' fridge. She sits at the kitchen table and drinks too quickly, thirstily, thinks that she needs more water, opens another beer instead.

Standing by the window, her hips pressed against the sink, she glances around the kitchen, reminds herself to wash the coffee mugs on the counter, to get rid of the rotten bananas in the fruit bowl. She sips and feels relaxed, watches the dogs chase bugs under the kumquat tree, flicks her eyes up, with some admiration, at the new, obese Tudor on the hill that used to be covered in forest. The Rosenblooms had disliked that house since the first surveyor appeared with his tripod and scanner. There is a figure in one of the windows, and Sandra is transfixed, unwilling to move, watching the person she imagines is also watching her. She feels like the women in the books she reads, about to fall toward something. So when she does turn from the window, she's merely closing a book: the story will wait for her return. She wants to share this with her students, to offer them these starring roles, this way out of their isolation.

She places the washed mugs in the drain tray and dries her hands on a dishtowel that smells faintly of mildew. Then she notices the black pickup in the driveway. Smoke escapes from the driver's tinted window, cracked open an inch. For a moment she is confused, wondering how long the truck has been there, if she should be dialing 911, but something about it looks familiar. When the driver steps out, she half-smiles—it's only Jesse. A self-described model who also sings in a band, he bounces back and forth from L.A. and always makes time for the Rosenblooms' odd jobs. He walks around to the kitchen entrance but doesn't come in. Sandra waits a beat then calls out, "Hello?"

He doesn't seem surprised to see her in the house, just tilts his head inside the screen door. "Do you smoke?" he says in greeting, and his lashes fall then rise slowly, settling on her face like she's sitting at a hotel bar, waiting for someone just like him.

It takes her a moment to disengage from that gaze, to realize he's offering marijuana, which she automatically declines. She drains the rest of her beer and reaches for another, tries to get back the cool, relaxed feeling she had a moment ago.

When he does come in, minutes later, he's careful not to let the screen door slam. He inspects the label on the bottle in her hand, goes straight for the fridge and takes one for himself, pulls out a chair at the wooden table and asks, "Do you mind...?" She shrugs, not sure how to respond.

It's not up to her to give permission. They are both hired help, equally entitled to occupy the house, each on their special assignments. But when he has another beer, and another, keeping up with her, she worries about the empties. If the Rosenblooms were to walk in unexpectedly, they would find her and Jesse alone in the house, neither one working at anything but instead getting high—their situation would be indefensible. Well, he does have a pleasing face, she admits. He probably gets the odd modeling job, but does he have any real talent? He has grown heavier since the last time she saw him, at the Rosenbloom fundraiser for a tree-planting organization, his neck and waist softer. This makes him only slightly less appealing, slightly less intimidating because of how he looks.

At the fundraising picnic she had excused herself from Marcus's side to wander through flower knots and up a dirt trail, seeking a view. She had run into Jesse and his friend, also with photogenic cheekbones, also in his twenties, and they had been sharing a joint. They were casual with her, waving her over and speaking polite nonsense, smiling at her with lazy, feline eyes. She had noticed the moon in the sky, odd to see it during the day, and then she had let them each kiss her goodbye before she turned and walked down the path to her husband. The kissing was cultural, she told herself, unsure if the custom was South American or European or what, exactly. She had kissed the friend first, and then Jesse, full on the lips, and they had taken their time, lingering and gentle with her. These were kisses that tasted uncommon and persuasive, like invitations. So unlike the measured, marital pecks that lately felt like insurance payments, these gave her a rush she replayed for days.

Jesse tells her he is here to do some painting, and then they sit in silence, drinking their beers. She remembers hearing something about a pregnant girlfriend, gossip at a baby shower, but she doesn't say anything. She knows it is incongruous for a person like her, a person who loves words, to hate using them, but she often does. She hates trying to make them deliver, unrehearsed, ideas that don't always sound like her own, feelings she doesn't yet understand.

When Jesse speaks, she's not sure she hears him correctly. Maybe he's talking to her in a foreign language, or else she is drunk-listening and the words have gone out of order. He looks first at her bare feet before raising his eyes to her face, before saying, as if he has just come up with the most irresistible idea ever: "Let's shower in the leaves." She feels instantly guilty, aware of how long she has been away from home, from Marcus. Like during that first, extra hour of Daylight-Saving Time, with her classes behind her, when she should be doing something unselfish like making dinner and then going for a walk with Marcus, but instead buries herself in a romance, occasionally glancing out the window at all that good light.

Even though it is not exactly clear what Jesse is inviting her to do, Sandra breathes in the scent of enticement that wafts from the envelope. It is so delicious to be tempted—she knows this from her novels—that she wants to prolong the feeling of temptation, the itch, though not until it necessitates scratching. She wants it both ways: the steady, dependable inside light and the newly abundant daylight. She wants her little gluttonies, like letting the hot shower run and run, cramming an entire cookie or cupcake into her mouth and savoring the sugar rush, cancelling her classes so she can stay in bed and read. This is the opposite of how Marcus does things.

Because she is not certain how to answer Jesse, she stares out the window, at the kumquat tree, at the leaves on the ground mixed with dog droppings, until their situation begins to lose its delicate, absurd intrigue. She'd rather imagine the figure from the Tudor's window beckoning to her, and herself walking over, up the wide, winding staircase to a fragrant bath and other pleasures, than run around with Jesse, naked—does he mean for them to be naked?—in the Rosenblooms' backyard. She thinks about Jesse touching her.

When she opens her eyes, he is slouching against the screen door, next to the washer and dryer, the huge bags of dog food.

"Wait here," he says, not moving toward her. "I'll show you."

She watches as he dumps the contents of Edda's laundry basket, her soiled stockings rolled into a mesh bag, her camel trousers and taupe cotton sweaters, and kicks them into a corner. He takes the basket outside and begins to fill it with leaves from beneath the kumquat tree.

Once again, unbidden, the image of her childhood friend, Angel, comes to her. Thirteen-year-old Angel, eighteen-year-old Angel— they're graduating from high school, no longer friends, but Sandra has heard the rumors and knows certain things. Good-girl Sandra is jealous of what Angel knows.

Sandra's sudden urge is to lock the door, run out the back, get in her Rabbit and drive home to her husband. Certainly Marcus is there waiting for her, willing to listen to her recap the day over a cocktail and some pretzels, or maybe he will agree to go to her favorite bistro and continue to get even sloppier on house wine. She stands too quickly, feeling the alcohol, and watches Jesse for a moment, his strong arms scooping up piles of leaves in the gorgeous failing light, and as she is entitled to do, as Angel would do, as any Cloquet heroine worth her embroidered silk bodice would do, slowly sits back down.

ANGEL

Florida, summer: it's eighty-five degrees with ninety percent humidity, and maybe, as her mother has counseled, Angel could be sympathetic toward her best friend's malaise, but Sandra is unreachable. Ever since the incident at the club, Sandra is basically wasting her final weeks before eighth grade, when they'll be queens of middle school, on soft-core romances that Angel has tried to read without getting past a page. And straight-A Sandra, of all people, knowing there are better books, sexier books, worth reading—books like *The Bell Jar,* tucked in Angel's bookbag, while the *Hardy Boys* take up an entire shelf in Sandra's bedroom, the kind of juxtaposition that makes Angel cringe.

How can Sandra stand those grimy paperbacks when there are library books, treasures for anyone to find, that will tear you up, like *1984*? Sandra would swoon over *The Lover*, so what if the librarian gives you a look, and *Blue Calhoun*, worth mucking through pages of yearning to get to the scenes of fornication. For a curious reader there are remarkable finds, *Tropic of Cancer* and *A Sport and a Pastime*, that show what you'll need to know soon enough. Under the title *Close-Ups*, there are more age-appropriate stories about getting so tan your features melt together and escaping luggish boyfriends Angel hasn't met yet.

Even if she wanted to remind Sandra of these books, it would be impossible since they no longer spend every day together. When Angel walks by Sandra's house, the garage door is open and Sandra's bike is missing; she is at Highland Pool where she lies for hours, inert, tanning and reading. To Angel, she is a blur, someone who moves in camouflage, who hides her real plans behind vague chatter. Sandra will disappear into middle school, high school, and then college, places from which unforgiven, former best friends are banished.

Before their separation, when they still belong to each other, they run out of school on the last day of seventh grade, hand in hand and screaming with joy. It's obvious to both of them that Angel is transforming, her hair swinging loose at her waist as if having grown overnight, her body becoming tall and thin while Sandra struggles against extra pounds. That Angel has bloomed in the way certain young girls do is evident by how men look at her, but men will look at anything, Sandra says. Angel waits impatiently for the end of June so she can turn fourteen, notices how strong yet slender her wrists and ankles are, encircled in brightly colored yarn, how long and graceful her fingers, especially when placed next to Sandra's squarish hands.

This summer, both girls are released from any set schedule. There is no swim class, no gymnastics, no Girl Scout camp. The parents are preoccupied with work and conjugal disturbances, aging, varying degrees of drinking. They want to believe that youth is carefree, so they hand over money to their children and hope for the best.

Angel and Sandra buy bus passes and go everywhere they can think of: the head shops and bikini boutiques of Coconut Grove, mini-golf next to the freeway, the dance club in Ft. Lauderdale where they stand outside the doors at eight o'clock at night and burn forbidden cigarettes, hoping to look older. There is one bouncer who will let them in, after which they make a pact to lose each other for one hour, no more. When they meet up again in the bathroom, they apply layers of Chapstick to puckered lips. They smile and save their stories for the walk to the bus stop, holding hands the whole time.

What have they been up to tonight, Sandra's mother asks when they return at ten thirty from the supermarket with brownie mix and smoke in their hair. Angel calls home to check in and says she can't really talk since she and Sandra are painting each other's nails. They underbake the brownies and eat them half-raw in the middle, the way they taste best. They think of themselves as good girls, but only half the time.

The other half they are doing bad girl things, like walking around the house in their skimpy bathing suits for the benefit of Sandra's older brother, who's rarely home, and going into his room to find his secret stash of magazines and drugs, pocketing two tabs of what must be acid—little squares of paper with yellow smiling faces printed on them. They put these under their tongues at the beach, and swim, and feel nothing.

"Fooled again," Sandra says, but an hour later, the visions come. Angel sees spiders, God-sized, expanding to fill the sky, and she gets chills in the sun-warm water. Everything is sharply beautiful, the shapes of bathers at the shoreline, the children, the seagulls and sandpipers, the way they all glow. Sand is a code: you can see how each grain adds up to a curving pink shell, a puzzle. Everything answers a question. When they get home, Sandra's mother is distracted by something, an argument with her ex-husband and then by how dinner turned out, and Angel is relieved that she doesn't notice their pupils like black holes. When Sandra announces they're going out, her mother asks only if they need more money. They are invincible, the most fearless girls ever. They look into the mirror to put on make-up, and their eyes suck up all the light until they can't believe how pretty they are. At the club, they get a lot of attention from boys who look like men, or men who act like boys, it's hard to tell the difference.

They are having the best time until the fight happens. Something is going on with Sandra's sister who is not a good girl, not even half the time, but Sandra refuses to say what it is. Angel's heart is swirling, her brain is stuck on sex and shimmer. She keeps asking for the details, but Sandra won't speak, and Angel can't comfort her, and they separate, go home on their own.

At the bus stop where Angel waits, the glass billboard is smashed, creating a jagged hole around the ad model's face. A boy standing next to her reaches into his jacket pocket and asks if she wants some. Chunks of glass glitter on the concrete. They walk to the beach, only a block away, and there is just enough wind to make them huddle in the sand to keep the joint lit.

It's exciting at first, kissing outside in the damp air, the way his hand moves against her bare back, under her t-shirt, the relaxed feeling like floating in the ocean. Then they are having sex, and she doesn't want to, but it happens so fast and she is not sure how to make him stop, simply asking seems weird. She tries to like how it feels, but it's different from the books she has read; she doesn't think he is nice anymore, and she is starting to hate herself. After a while he finishes and gets in a hurry to leave. She searches in the sand but can't find the little woven bag that holds her money and bus pass. She walks the three miles home by herself, thinking mostly about what she will say to Sandra. Then, what a stupid thing she has done. And a kind of elation, for having done it. She is still wearing her night eyes, but her chest is tight. There is sand stuck to her arms and legs, so she picks at it, grain by grain, like picking off tiny scabs.

Sandra finally tells Angel that her sister was raped. At night, while
waiting for the bus in Hialeah. Now Angel can't tell her own story even
if it's close to or maybe the same thing. She can't tell anyone, either to
boast or get help, but by the end of summer she has tested negative
with three pregnancy kits and stops worrying.

In September, in homeroom, she sees her classmates differently, the
ones she has known since elementary school when they walked home
together and stopped at Seven-Eleven for cinnamon Jolly Ranchers
and peanut butter Chick-O-Sticks—they're still little kids with untied
shoelaces and crusts of sleep in the corners of their eyes. In English they
discuss irony, and her perfect example is how she can't say anything to
Sandra while a total stranger at the teen health clinic can watch her, naked
from the waist down, to ensure she correctly inserts her new, peach-
colored diaphragm. She wants to tell Sandra that sex feels like power, like
revenge. Armed and dangerous, she has slept with two high school boys
by Thanksgiving, has fooled around with Sandra's brother during winter
break, and since New Year's is seeing Drew, one of the lifeguards who
watched over Sandra during those weeks in August when Angel became a
nonentity, when Sandra disappeared into her romance novels and got so
tan her cheeks, nose, and mouth became indistinguishable.

By now, especially after the brother thing, she and Sandra are officially
over. Before that they drift awhile, together less and less often because
Sandra has new rules to be home by ten, even on weekends. Sandra
becomes Honor Club vice president, makes the cheerleading squad, and
gets new friends who are the girls she and Angel used to ignore.

Angel lets boys take up her free time, all the planning to meet
when parents aren't around. She likes the messiness of them, the
evidence they leave behind: dirty underclothes and tangled hair, the
imprint of the safety belt against her back. The boys like her because
she doesn't make them work too hard, but then they brush her off
for the same reason.

She would like to tell Sandra the details. She would like to go
over how it feels, moment by moment, how her chest and neck and

eyes grow hot, how exciting it is to know all the adult things worth knowing. She would like to say it is exactly as they talked about, that she feels wide awake, all senses alive like the wolf in the wisdom deck she shoplifted from the Cryptic Crystal at the mall. She would like to, but she can't remember what she does when she is usually so drunk or stoned that it seems like something she dreamed. Even with Drew, who has his own apartment, more or less, in his parents' garage, she can only ever say how it starts, a six-pack and his black cobra bong on the fruit crate that serves as a coffee table, the television playing with the sound off, her cheek resting against his thigh. And then it is one in the morning, and he is pushing her out the door.

"Boys are such beasts," Sandra might say. But now that Angel has seen inside their bathrooms, their closets, she is no longer mystified by the way boys are. Instead, she desperately wants to know how she is supposed to be when she is with them. Is it okay to be repulsed and attracted at the same time? Is it okay that it still hurts, at first, for a while, and that she fights against them to make it feel better, to make it feel, finally, almost good? These are not questions she can talk about with Drew. It is easier, each time, to keep drinking until everything melts away.

The four years of high school seem endless. Before blowing out the candles on her eighteenth birthday cake, Angel wishes she could feel some pride about keeping her grades up and getting accepted into a small local college. She is not going to the opposite end of the country, all the way to California, like Sandra, but at least she won't feel like a junior college joke. Rather than get on the waitlist for campus housing, she searches the *Sarasota Sun* and arranges to share an apartment with two other girls. She hasn't seen Sandra all summer, so when she hears a knock on her parents' door a week before classes start, she is surprised to see her old friend standing there like a bashful date, holding a cluster of dyed-pink daisies wrapped in green tissue paper.

This image sticks with her, and she relies upon it when she's dancing. She hasn't felt authentically shy about anything for a long time, so it helps to picture what shy looks like when she removes her clothes for strangers and tries to give off girl-next-door vibes. She is a night girl whose only inconvenience is sharing the dressing room with the departing day shift. One girl is always in the shower, steaming up the mirrors and singing; she drives a hyper-accessorized, bubblegum-pink Honda and always takes home gifts, a tub of Red Vines, a small plush bear wearing a silver bracelet around its neck. Alternatively, the girl in Goth makeup who can do a vertical split, and her sidekick, the underage-looking one who sometimes dates the DJ, gripe about how slow it's been. Nobody's coming in during the day because it's Christmas, these two complain, because it's Valentine's, Easter, summer. Because of the too-high cover. Because the free lunch sucks. Because it's raining.

At first Angel is a weekends-only day girl, so she sees them regularly, the reluctant ones, huddled under boyfriend jackets in the air-conditioned cold and casting hostile eyes at the robust blondes (Pink Honda) who monopolize groups of customers with dance after dance, keeping them on edge, keeping the party going. A bitter day girl always breaks down and breaks her boyfriend's rule, asks the lone guy in the third row to the VIP, how else is she going to pay rent? She gets up close as he unbuttons his pants and sometimes begs her to touch it—she hates it when they beg. There are cameras and she's unsure who's watching, but she's excited, now, about the money. Outside the curtain, she reluctantly peels off the house's share from her clutch of twenties; the customer is gone and she spends the rest of the afternoon waiting around for nothing, sullen day girl. The blondes are now working in pairs, entertaining a new group of guys, and later, standing at the bar and swallowing large mouthfuls of thickly sauced pasta, these stars make a performance of paying their stage fees like it's nothing, casually pulling a few big bills out of their stuffed shoulder bags. All this is child's play compared to what shows up after ten p.m., the cocaine and heroin and businessmen who are professional negotiators. Still, the evening pickings are so much easier. Some of the day girls stay on, some have to be home by dinnertime. Some of them will be punished either way.

Angel has no such limitations and classes four days a week. She dances for fun, not out of necessity; she switches to nights because that's when someone interesting might walk in. She has every intention of getting her degree and then who knows, she could apply to law school, look up Sandra in California. She has seen the pre-law types at the college, the men especially who already wear their suits like they know they're going to win at everything. Right now her life is as clear and methodical as a board game—black square, white square. She can move back and forth with impunity.

One night while it is still early, Angel is bored. She digs into the lost-and-found bin, seeking the best articles for her send-up of the nervous, auditioning newb: the girl who gets so drunk that she can barely find the pole. The bin is full of torn tube dresses, discarded panties, and perspired-in shoes, but Angel finds the perfect mismatched pieces, applies exaggerated makeup, and staggers onto the stage. The routine is hilariously authentic, everyone nearly falls off his chair laughing, and she is tipped exceptionally well. Afterward, Bridget comes over to the table where Angel is sitting with three men who keep buying her drinks. Bridget offers them a lap dance, two-on-one times three—both girls with each customer. It is during these dances, as their group gets progressively rowdier and raunchier, that Bridget wraps her long, silky arms around Angel's waist and pulls her into the inner circle.

The circle is a place of acquisitions and mergers. So-and-so could use a girl for an evening, a week, a month, and the girl could use a wealthy boyfriend, could use the rent, the dinners out, the new outfits. A less-than-divine balance is achieved—so-and-so has unusual tastes; voilà, here's Mystique who spent most of her childhood chained to a bed. Angel has glimpsed these arrangements without interest until it comes to Bridget, who bends to her the way she herself bent for so many boys, laying her head in their unresisting laps. It's beyond awesome to think Bridget could be her girlfriend.

She has watched so many times as Bridget, now her roommate, too, slides to the floor with her hands gripping the pole behind her head,

moves her thighs apart sooo slowly it's as if she is underwater, invites
a long, hushed look at what is partially visible beneath the disco party
lights. When Bridget is not busy in the VIP room, Angel stands with
a drink and watches, mesmerized by Bridget's beauty. Heat rises from
Bridget's skin like a vapor; men in work-worn clothes, in pressed suits,
in Hawaiian shirts sit with their alcohol and free burgers, appetite and
privation congealing in their oil-black eyes.

Early in the morning Bridget falls into bed giggling, drops five
hundred dollars on Angel's bare stomach.

"You won't believe it," she says. "We're in Denny's. He orders for
me—pancakes, fruit bowl, bacon, coffee, eggs. He hands me a laxative.
He makes me eat all the toast, with butter and jam. Orange juice. He
says, 'Go now. Use the last stall and don't flush.' It takes a while, but I
do it, you know? When I come back, he gets up. He's got this look on
his face, like…heaven. He puts the money on the table in front of me
and heads back there; he never even touches me. I swear, the first time
I met him, I could smell something on his breath. Not ordinary rotten,
something else. You could come with me, the next time. He'll triple this."

Angel pushes the money aside and gets up, starts rapidly brushing
her hair. After a few minutes, she throws the brush at Bridget. It
hits Bridget in the forehead, near her hairline, and she bleeds. Angel
wonders if the exhilaration she feels after hurting Bridget is anything
like so-and-so's joy, if the look on her face is similar to the look on his.
Bridget's freckled, Teflon skin will scab then reveal a bright pink circle
that rapidly pales to strawberry-and-cream perfection.

Bridget can be magnificent, a white-booted majorette. She
wears bruises like rosettes, from spiraling the pole, from after-hours
customers. By the time Portia is born, she has saved enough to put a
down payment on a house.

"You can visit us every day," she says to Angel. "You can sleep over
on weekends."

Alone in their apartment, Angel tells herself a story: she is hurrying across a new campus, late for the mock trial she has volunteered to jury. She is not a law student, not yet. She has a receptionist job in a small firm but comes to the college on weekends, orders her coffee short in a tall cup at the café that is busy with graduate students, pretends to be one of them. She hasn't looked for Sandra since she moved out here, but she trusts they'll find each other eventually. It would be nice to know how Sandra is doing, if they could be friends again.

Navigating with to-go cup in one hand and notebook in the other, she run-walks a long concrete hallway, keeps checking the room number scrawled on her wrist. A man stands in the doorway she is to enter. His nametag says *Ever So Dreamy*, and he is clean-suited and smiling so hard she glances down to make sure she hasn't spilled her coffee. She hasn't.

This will happen. It's got to.

A GOOD LIFE

WITHOUT OVERTHINKING it, Cat decided on Ocean, the young Welsh poet, the same way she decided this was what most Colony residents did with their spare time—each other. She had chosen him before he even arrived, based on his bio. When he turned out to be zealous about reciting his original verse while seated on crossbeams or tree limbs, she liberated her own reserves of charm.

On Friday night, as she climbed the porch to after-dinner charades, he called from the steps below, "I apotheosize the globes of your thighs!" What a relief. A tryst with Ocean might ease the sting of being politely disinvited from ever again having brain-churning, rapt-soul sex with the Famous Irish Novelist, who had returned to his wife and informed Cat in a typed letter.

The Famous Irish Novelist's words delivered calamity and clarity. After reading them once, Cat understood her new prerogative: to have whatever sex she could negotiate, as many times as was feasible, with Ocean, and then later, hopefully soon, with Chance Thomas, the Southern fiction writer. That she had accepted the position of residency intern at the same golden artists' retreat where her Famous Irish Novelist had resided, on the edge of the Pacific, was a scary freedom.

Before her were mostly unplanned days, weeks, and months that might feel full of promise one minute and pointless the next, an aggregate of exhilaration and anxiety that had already invaded her dreams. What she had, whether she wanted it or not, was the Famous Irish Novelist's— Flynn's—ghost in the cool wisps of morning and the endless hours of night. She had his flannel shirt, too, covered in dog hair and smelling like his medieval home, mostly, just a little of him left in the arms and collar. She had the boys around her, new boys every six weeks, and Lulu, and all the time she needed to create her magnum opus.

She and Lulu had hit it off so completely they couldn't believe their good luck, and while the Colony stipend was minimal, their duties were few; they were freed from real-job restrictions and had time to work on whatever they liked. Here, Flynn had drafted what would become his first bestseller. Here, his wife, the infamous fabric designer Naomi Mirkin, had initiated, via her series of sustainably plant-sourced, biodegradable forms, the far-reaching social art movement known as Dismirkining. Maybe Cat and Lulu could make their names here, too.

Cat hadn't shared her envisioned masterwork, THINK U R FLY, with anyone but Lulu. The installation, once complete, would consist of a 35 mm film reel with seams showing *equal to* the buzzy itch of vinyl *equal to* the emotional mercury of graffiti *equal to* the impression of a body, hers, rising, falling, vanishing, and reappearing between towering trees. She could already see the gallery set-up, her film jumping from large white wall to large white wall over a soundtrack of cicadas. The shrieking of their sawing wings would get progressively louder—entire walls of sound moving back and forth in a call-and-response rhythm— and then the room would go dark and silent. Cat imagined that the absence of visual and aural stimuli would paralyze the visitors for a full minute, would suspend them in a state that would feel like fear or relief, before the loop of film and noise started over from the beginning. She would create an experience that kept starting and stopping and starting, that almost didn't hurt.

Early Friday morning, she and Lu had dropped the artists off in the affluent downtown before picking up their own supplies. They drove to Lu's city studio and moved most of Lu's sculpture equipment, including chunks of steel and an oxygen/acetylene set, into the Colony pickup. After stopping at the local hardware store for Cat's pine lumber and nylon rope, they unloaded everything at the Colony barn and went back down to retrieve the artists, who had stocked up on ibuprofen, chocolate, postcards, Blackwing pencils, and a locally made bread stuffed with artichokes. They took a short break before dinner—Lulu mowed the lawn and Cat lay on her bed, thinking. Then there was fish or tempeh, potatoes, and salad, prepared by the Colony chef, and wine and beer, and game night, which seemed to go on forever.

Under the new moon, Cat waited impatiently for the artists to return to their studios, watched their flashlights bob drunkenly across the dark grass. Then she followed Ocean to his writer's cottage, let the door flap behind them. She barely felt the doorknob punch her spine before she lunged, all hot potato, into his arms.

She knew—of course she knew—this had also been Flynn's little house. Her heart retreated slightly, but the crotch rocking and glute grabbing had begun, a game of Twister playing out fast like a scene about sex, so she stayed to watch what would happen next. She liked Ocean's body, liked his enthusiasm and athleticism, and yet, unlike Flynn, Ocean had not experienced sufficient deprivation, compromise, and failure to fully appreciate Cat's newness, to exaggerate her ability to bring him hope. She herself was too new to think this way, to understand what was absent between them. After, in his boyish, uncertain way, Ocean might ask Cat how she was doing. Flynn wouldn't waste words on her imagined condition; he would see her exactly as she was.

While their sweat dried, Ocean vaped, blew berry-scented smoke out of the tiny window, and wrote in his spiral notebook. Cat rummaged through her feelings, hoped they'd have another go. But her thoughts wandered: which paint color should she and Lulu use on the artists' doors—Moon Bisque or Garnet Mirage? The cottages had been cerulean during Flynn's month, she knew, for he had described them to her. *Sky opened to more sky.* During Naomi Mirkin's residence there had been no cottages or doors, just the original barn and shoji screens.

At last Ocean put down his writing and they entwined again, this time more slowly, capturing something authentic that a camera could follow in a long take, a liquid spark that lit and fused, water into sand. The night passed in a looping pop song. Cat was grateful not to dream about Flynn.

In the morning the room was heavy with fog, the window latch still unhinged from the night before. Her brain brushed against Flynn's letter, the other items he had returned to her, *for protection*, as if he and she were driving in opposite directions to avoid ending up in the same prison. Cat could have wept, but she and Lu had their handmaidens' pact: never let them see you wallow, or more succinctly, *sub the blub.* Subbing, Cat eased out of Ocean's warm, damp bed and somnambulated over thicket and bramble to gather Lulu for the People's Art Walk. Still subbing, Cat lightly checked Ocean off her list.

At the main gate, Roy pushed the last hay bale, improvised seating, into the bed of the pickup, the sun beginning to burn coastal condensation into fairy dust.

"Might yet be a warm one," he said, hands patting tires and combing over fuses, grooming the well-used truck as if she were a thoroughbred. Cat shivered, squinching her face toward the promised light and heat.

In Doc Martens and a Motörhead t-shirt knotted above the bellybutton, Lulu kicked dirt. Cat stared at Lu's brave, bare belly, the enameled daisy that pierced her navel and jumped on its tiny gold chain. Their eyes met: *Stop. Thinking. About. Him.* Between them, there were too many hims.

"Womyn," Roy announced, ready to get going, "She's gassed and shoed, needs saddled-up with two Igloos, inch from the top in ice and bug juice, as per usual. Looks like we're brim with townies today and like-ass-not some last-minute wanna-goes, one never knows." These were lined up in the grass parking lot behind the entry gate: grandparents from Palo Alto, a sun-bleached hipster from Half

Moon Bay, a quartet of Castro leatherbears, and a trio of Noe Valley
roommates. At the last minute, as Roy had predicted, a couple pulled
up in an RV with Iowa plates. Cat and Lu fed the garden hose into the
jugs, stirred in the blue chemical sugar that passed for drink, counted
out the sandwiches.

"Can we talk later," Lulu said, chewing the inside of her cheek.

"Okay," Cat said, scared for someone's heart.

At almost nine, the sun still working on the fog, their group
was arranged as comfortably as possible in the back of the truck.
Cat and Lulu crammed into the front seat, their closeness agitating,
unreasonably, Cat's sense of doom. As they lurched over gopher
mounds and spider holes, a soul-crunching dread sprang its claws:
Cat was going to have to pretend, again, to appreciate all the art.

She told herself not to say anything, simply to smile serenely
and let Roy do his tour guide magic. But as soon as they parked,
led everyone through the wooden horse gate and around bursts of
poison oak toward their first stop, she groaned. This piece was the
worst: a nude, zaftig female carved out of petals of soda-can aluminum
and hammered—hammered!—into the trunk of a California oak.
Trees and their wood were primary components of all the art pieces,
and maybe this one was a feminist statement, but to Cat it looked
like rusted junk, an insult if not an actual injury to the tree. Lady
Godiva symbolized everything the seventies *hadn't* achieved—equality
for women, reproductive freedom via a cancer-causing pill, the
oxymoronic idea of free love. No-good-goddess-goes-unpunished.
Cat felt the old resentment sting her like a plastering of burrs: she and
Lu were good enough to serve the residents but not good enough to be
awarded the gift of residency. She must have muttered these thoughts
out loud because she felt Lu's glare deliver a two-fingered *thwap!*
against her forehead.

Soon enough they were moving toward exhibit number two,
the Beer Chimes inside the hollowed atrium of a charred redwood.
Following the path Roy had cleared the day before, they passed a
monstrous fig tree with limbs ripe for climbing. This was Cat's hiding

tree, one she claimed for wasting time, lying on her back above the creek with arms and legs dangling into pleasant, buzzing numbness. She felt Flynn come over her then, the sorghum of his voice reading to her parts of his novels, not crude so much as visceral with unguarded stares, childish mouth breathing, the intentional loosening of fabric, unsubtle revelations of skin.

A straw fedora poked through the branches, and she started—Flynn? as if she had desired him into being—but it was just Mr. Half Moon Bay, using the wilds to obey his prostate.

She looked around guiltily, saw Lulu doing their job for both of them, corralling the group toward the tree gutted by fire, encouraging each guest to step all the way inside for a moment, to tap the brown glass chimes with a fingertip and imagine the juxtaposed cacophony of the burning forest.

"Spoiled," Lulu whispered. "You have an entire Ocean and all you do is pine."

Spoiled, Cat thought of Chance, the Southern story writer, how she had driven him into town at his request, just the two of them, how she had struggled with the Colony Honda's manual transmission. How he had said, matter-of-factly, "Grab it like a dick," and how this had worked, plus made her like him even more for revealing what she thought of as his libertine side. And then the party last week, all of them racing around the barn, wild-footed after sharing a bottle of Jäger, and herself, in her ever-present camera eye, gaining speed and approaching lift-off, convinced she looked like a modern dance nymph with Chance at her back but never close enough to mingle sweat. Chance telling her, as they passed within an inch of one another, "Damn, your vortex."

What to do with this need for love, for being loved, for Flynn, who was, right then, probably eating dinner with Naomi Mirkin and their too-handsome, straight-A sons, passing around butter for the potatoes, salt for the lamb chops, and, as a condiment, Naomi's homemade mint jelly, the way she could transform herbaceous plants while Cat fumbled the gear shift, pulled into the post office parking lot and waited like an overheated dog for Chance to mail his prose to editors on both coasts along with a fat, handwritten letter and package—earrings he had offered for Cat's approval—to his longtime girlfriend who would eventually become his wife.

In the woods, the next stop a welcome distraction, Cat got her camera ready. If she had to name a favorite, this piece was it: a broken necklace of huge redwood beads scattered down the hillside. Some were blackened all over, always the specter of California wildfires, but unlike the burnt-out chimney tree, here she found the artist's story compelling. Some beads were smooth and round or shellacked and cylindrical, some were rough-hewn and square. Most were designed with grooved centers that invited visitors to settle and contemplate. She snapped a nice series of photos, five seated guests and the remainder standing between the trees on unlevel planes, each in their own thoughts about their proximity to the giant scarred jewels, all having their rockstar moment.

Flynn had given her a necklace made of tiny metal and semiprecious stones strung on a waxed cord that absorbed the scent of her perfume, her skin. After a rare, entire day together, he had pulled her hair aside to disentangle it from the clasp and bitten her shoulder, drawing blood. For her, this had been the epitome of their love.

"Are your tummies a-rumblin', audacious art addicts? Fear not—or fear some—for as contractually obligated, we'll be bringing 'round your light repast to exhibit number four, the Easter Amphitheater," Roy announced, the girls' signal to unload the provisions. Cat salivated a little at the thought of their midday reward, chicken sandwiches and icy grape soft drink.

Lu stayed quiet as they jogged the shortcut back to the truck; they had only fifteen minutes before the tour humped its way to the grove. She didn't fight Cat for the driver's seat, didn't noodle with her usual advice about looking over one's shoulder before backing up or how Cat should try the road this time instead of throwing them blindly across the grass. Outside of the forest, as Roy had predicted, the day was hot and humid. Sea currents fed the wicked thistles that would grow to six feet, tall as Flynn, by summer's end. Bearing seductive purple flowers, these spiraled up like weapons, so drenched in boils, spikes and spiny whiskers that getting close enough to tear them down seemed impossible.

"Lu, does he…" Cat asked uncertainly, eyes glued to the road, suddenly treacherous with sharp rocks and thick, black mud. Despite the sun, every living thing was holding on to its damp, primordial beginnings, and Lulu was right there, fat tears dropping into her lap, soft slugs darkening her jeans.

"I'm going to have his baby, I'm going to. But if he won't…" Lulu had one good man, maybe, and a tiny, beating heart that took its strength, seven weeks now, she had figured, from her abundance. They were attached deeper than anything she had ever known, so like her skin, her lungs, her blood that she could no sooner let go than cut her own wrists. Cat knew this and envied her. "Fuck it, Cat, what am I supposed to do? Show up doublewide in August and start planning the honeymoon? I don't even know—" she was sobbing now. Cat steered the truck around a cavernous pothole, both hands fused to the wheel as the tires lost traction. Then they were flying, up over a hidden, felled trunk, some burnt-out redwood carcass that splintered even as it threw them into the air, a few inches but enough to make them scream for the ground, which caught them, seconds passing, or just the longest half-second on record. They sank down, firm in the grip of the sucking wet dirt.

"Goddamn it!" Cat cried, flinging her hands from the steering that had paid little attention to her.

Lulu coughed up a jagged laugh, the adrenaline working to even out her sadness. "I bet you wish you got that on film," she gasped.

They peered into the truck bed and inspected the damage: one juice cooler had come unlatched and was emptying its sticky contents onto the ground, but the lunches, smartly packed in a heavy-duty trash bag, were unharmed. Lulu maneuvered sideways and slapped the Igloo's lid into place while Cat flipped on the engine, pressed her foot to the gas. They sat there, going nowhere.

"Goddamn," Cat said again. "Why does *everything* feel so stuck?" By everything, she mainly meant Flynn.

The night Cat and Flynn began, the night she had stayed after his reading in the city and thrilled when he invited her to coffee, she watched him watch her, his enigmatic smile, as she drank and ate with real thirst and hunger. When she came up for breath, he had touched her, brushed an invisible crumb from her chin so that she was no longer able to press her lips back together, couldn't swallow the moist, half-chewed cud of cookie pocketed in her cheek.

He had said, in his most deliberately accentuated brogue, "If you keep using your beauty as an excuse, you will get fucked," and the words burned into her brain, but she couldn't respond because he had moved his chair next to hers so that the backs overlapped, creating a semi-private room. He might have said, *if you keep using your youth as an excuse*, but she preferred to remember it the first way, her desire to hear the word *beauty* paralyzing, almost shameful. He had reached his hand under her skirt in the most gentle, obscene way she had imagined she wanted him to, had entered her then, in public, without asking, the fingers of his other hand still grasping her chin and pressing so forcefully against her mouth that she wasn't sure if he wanted to slap her or kiss her the way she was begging him to in her head, *kiss me don't hurt me*, her armpits damp then trickling sweat under her t-shirt, the bra she hadn't worn, the beauty or youth that had turned itself against her just as he had promised.

Lu threw open the door of the cab and stared at the sludge, gave up and jumped into it, crouched to peer at the truck's underside, stood, stared some more. Cat felt stupid, devoid of helpful suggestions, emotionally infused with a primal fight-or-flight response that could bring on a spastic fit or sometimes, irrationally, an attack of sleep. She yawned several times in a row, like hiccups, her hysteria rising.

"We're fucking stuck, and someone has to go to the barn and get help, someone has to tell Roy lunch will be late, maybe cut the tour short," Cat sputtered, yawning compulsively. "And then he's going to kill us."

"No fucking way," Lulu argued. She climbed back into the cab and dug around, muck-covered boots in the air, came up with a burlap sack.

She ordered Cat to gather thistle stalks, rocks, anything halfway dry, and Cat did as she was told, happy to be of use. "Stomp it down," Lu ordered, and Cat did, creating a kind of platform behind the rear tires.

Lulu took her throne in the driver's seat, gunned the engine and again, louder, until smoke fell out the back like blood, the juice barrels cowering. The tires kicked up a hair and settled back into the ooze. Cat made as if to drag her feet in the direction of the barn.

"Get behind me now and push hard as you never thought you could," Lu commanded, and Cat knew she didn't have the muscle, but she placed her hands on the bumper anyway. Lulu threw the truck into low gear and hit the gas like she would kick it dead if it didn't play nice. Mud slammed Cat in the face, punched her in the stomach. She held on, no help at all, the rearview reflecting Lu's jaw set in a cold grimace, her body rocking back and forth with furious energy as if she could heave the beast forward by heart's desire alone.

The tires came loose all at once, easy and euphoric with release, like baby teeth. Lu roared forward onto a drier part of the road, kept the engine going as Cat ran to catch up.

"He'd be a fool not to," Cat said too softly for Lulu to hear, and pulled the door closed with a thud. She wanted to laugh like crazy, to scream away her own heartache, to tell Lulu to drive through the gate and down the mountain, into the city and straight to Lu's apartment, to push Lu out and into the arms of her nice man, to tell him he had to love Lu because Lu was endlessly lovable and sometimes people needed to act grown up and do the thing they feared most, had to believe they were going to turn out all right. Then Cat would hold them tight, all of them together with the baby inside Lu, and she would know how it felt to join lives with the one you wanted, how Lulu and her baby and her man, plus their cat mewling in the apartment, would be a place to put Cat's feeling that she couldn't unhitch from Flynn.

They chugged their puny load to the grove, Lulu navigating and staying mad. Cat reached over to pet her arm, but Lu shrugged her off.

At last, their group munching contentedly, Roy made a point of bending both eyelids at the truck's disarray; mercifully, he skipped the interrogation. Cat wandered through the rows of seating, subbing hard, searching for something to clean the mess off her clothes. She thought about the Eastern Amphitheater's artist, Fatima, who had chosen to construct her outdoor temple in this specific location because it felt innately holy. Circular groups of benches imitated the grove of redwoods, and after lunch, they would march the group up the slight hill into the family of trees. Only by looking down from that elevated angle was it possible to see that the central row had originally spelled out the words, *have a good life*.

But the temple feet had been allowed to decay, in accord with the green vision embraced by Naomi Mirkin and shared by all the Colony artists of her period—signed into contract, as the history went, with menstrual blood and ejaculate on hemp parchment—so that the central queue now pronounced, *he ago lie*. Cat and Lulu had figured out some of the other phrases that could have emerged, ranging from the politic to the nonsensical: *hag lie, veg life, a goof, vag oodl if*—there was no way to predict how the pews would erode unless, again according to rumor, Fatima had abetted the process with critical cuts to the wood.

Then they were finishing up and about to be herded to the final, inevitable stop on the tour, Mirkin's installation. Spoiled, immature, cruel—all the self-deprecating, but accurate, epithets came to Cat as she grabbed spent napkins and sandwich boxes from the black nail-polished and garden-fortified fingers that offered these up helpfully. Cat punched the trash bag between deposits.

"Whoa, Psycho, what did the paper cup ever do to you?" Lulu whispered into her ear.

Cat stomped the bag down with a satisfying crunch as she compacted the remains. "Just want everything to take up as little space as possible, cradle to cradle, doing my job." She paused to apply lip gloss, breathed in the rejuvenating smell of bubblegum, threw the bag over her shoulder and put on her best I-may-look-daft-but-I'm-not face—cheeks sucked in, eyes wide, lips pushed out in a half-sneer. Lulu shook her head.

"You're kinda scaring me," Lu said, following Roy. When they reached the Mirkin Haus, Ocean was waiting for them, smiling. Cat stood with feet apart and didn't smile back, didn't put down the bag.

Roy explained that Mirkin had designed the structure, minus the anthropophagus witch, hellooo! as a gingerbread-style home, a secret place in the woods for lost children. Since no photographs existed, the group had to imagine its original form. One wall remained, an amalgam of boards contorted by sun, rain, and wind into ashen-colored spikes. A wad of lichen clung to the yawn of a splintered window frame, perhaps. Fossilized bits of color hinted at a mosaic path of barley-sugar that had spooled out from the front door.

Roy said that Mirkin's work was an exercise in time-lapse, in memory, in *her*story, that they were witnesses at a gravesite and birthplace simultaneously. After Roy spoke, as if on cue, Ocean mounted a tree that leaned over the Mirkin ruins and howled a poem, one of his own, to applause. For Cat, Ocean's lyrical shipboard romance with its fluttering, handkerchiefed farewell evoked yet another epoch of pretended enlightenment that had ended badly. She couldn't let the tour wrap up on the same false note as it had begun.

"Hey, y'all," Cat jumped in, some Southern haunt from Chance's part of the country creeping into her, joking with her voice box, making Lu look over her shoulder in horror.

"NO," Lulu mouthed, and Cat stared into her eyes, heard her silent words: *Not when they're all glad about their good time, their productive day of learning, their re-connect to the Mother.* But something had broken through, something was about to emerge. *I'm having a spiritual emergency,* Cat thought happily, hysterically.

"Do you *know* what a merkin is, people?" She felt free to say whatever came into her head, truly liberated by everything they had been admiring—if nature could turn art to shit and they could still call it art, if Naomi's sticks and stones were an elevated illustration of this, then they were all artists—creating, destroying, ad infinitum. She continued to speak, driven to see the group's reaction.

"Merkin: the next time your favorite clean-shaven porn star sports a seventies patch over her bikini wax, you'll be looking at one."

She crowed and swung the trash bag over her head. The Noe Valley contingent snickered, arm in arm, but a squall crossed Roy's brow.

"LuCat, bring up the truck, girls, before the damp completely rots what's left of your faculties."

Cat whooped some more, streaked with mud and Kool-Aid, glossed lips shining in the late afternoon light, wishing Flynn could see her. He'd likely think her daft, but he was missing out, wasn't he, on all her beautiful, youthful wildness.

Before dusk that evening, she sprinted into the woods. She had her video camera and the coil of nylon rope in her backpack, and she ran by every thistle copse, creek run-off and abandoned bird nest they'd passed earlier. At the Mirkin clearing, she threw the rope over a couple of tree limbs and tied knots to hold back the slippage, to create proper footholds for speed, for flight. She clamped the camera down, switched it on, and set to swinging.

With the camera recording, she felt strong and secure, witnessed. Wearing Lulu's cowhide welding gloves, holding the rope with both hands, feet resting in secure double loops like stirrups, she began moving through the trees. Her sneakers skimmed the dirt during the quickest run of the cord, and she kicked the ground, swinging up, then pushed back against a trunk to gain momentum. Her flying plan was to tie a hundred ropes like this one, and in her masterwork, Cat would break with gravity: she would fly through the forest like a new kind of human.

But tonight, she needed only one rope. She had purposefully set up her flight test in the trees that surrounded the Mirkin artwork, and she swooped over it with purpose, now, her feet touching down, her torso heaving forward. She breathed the cooling air, glass shards in her lungs, felt her heart jump out of her chest and propel itself thousands of miles, thrust itself through Flynn's ribcage. Gasping and dragging, she saw the steady, pulsing light on her camera recording her knotted rope, the darkening sky, the complicated, primitive effort required to get off the ground.

Flynn's final letter had arrived in a box with their other letters, photos, a mixtape, and several impractical love tokens Cat had sent him—salts for baths untaken, candles for nights unspent. The letter was brief but exacting, a ledger detailing what he had done to her, what she had done to him. She read it once, then tore his words into strips and burned these, putting one of the candles to use. She was not surprised, just furious at her own idiocy. Flynn's methods of persuasion, his practiced and versatile mental and emotional arsenals, were everything awful that drew her to him, were everything that made him indestructible.

Pulling hard on the rope, she rose and punted from hip to toe in a field-goal-worthy arc. Her sneaker snagged on a grasping maw of half-rotten leaves and branches, but she fought back. Her legs fired bolts of Nike's lightning, green at the edges where shame and fury converged, where the longing to do, to be something exceptional won out over good sense. Flying, Cat kicked and thrashed at the Mirkin remains the way nature would have done if it brought the storms they had out East; flying, she delivered the kind of aesthetic wallop Naomi believed in. Flying, she saw a halo of light through cracked lids and lowered lashes and something the brain did that was explained by science but that she couldn't explain, only feel imprinted on the insides of her body like new shoots of life.

RIPPLE

SEVERAL WEEKS after we get the news, my husband decides to throw a dinner party. At eighty-eight, his father has spots on lung and liver, and nobody says, "I'm sorry." Instead, their heads bob awkwardly as if in agreement. Frank was a seasoned smoker by age sixteen, the same year he was charged with possession and chose the Army over extradition to Mexico, the way he tells it. It's hard to know how to feel.

"The old man always pulls through," Dev says. "What we need is a jubilee." He looks good saying it, close-cropped beard accentuating dark eyes that flash with purpose for the first time since Sue's call. "You're both hot Cancerians, so let's steam crab."

I enjoy hearing my husband strive for wit.

"And for dessert, a soufflé—light as a cloud and easy on the teeth." It's hard to believe that the invincible Frank is taking a step back with each herb and citrus fruit, fat and acid we mark on the shopping list, which Dev has titled, "The Frank and Dev Show." He is so proud of himself, I don't tell him this sounds like a surefire bad idea.

Ten years prior, in the early 1990s, Devin and I are incommunicado with the family, heading for, in the middle of, or returning from a

Grateful Dead concert. Popular media promises that the nineties will turn the sixties on its ass, and we have been waiting our whole short lives to be part of the ripple effect. We travel whenever we can: to the Sam Boyd Silver Bowl, Autzen Stadium, Oakland Coliseum.

Our favorite is Las Vegas, where we get stoned and reverent and roam the halls of Caesar's Palace. We perceive special effects that aren't, really, are suckers for the carpets with repeating patterns of diamonds and jokers, the roulette wheels that yoo-hoo with vibraphone glissandos and expanding, circular rainbows. I find a corner-facing blackjack slot, win and lose the same twenty dollars for hours, while Devin's pupils dilate beside brightly dressed players at the craps table. He knows when the dice are going his way by the way they shine. Afterward, we drive to the Bowl, flying.

Now I open our driveway to Green Apple KinderCare traffic at 6:30 a.m. and watch parents project the appearance of calm. As they drop off their children, we manage minute-long conversations about bullying, outrageous internet memes, grandparents on perpetual cruises, too much fire, never enough rain. Today I take an informal poll: death date—to know or not to know?

"It might help to know," one cop dad, perplexed and generous with his ADHD son, admits. A meticulously resurfaced QVC model agrees; she could plan to spend her final weeks in a favorite ashram, alone! Only one mom marvels why I would ask such a thing in front of the children.

We don't see it at the time, but Devin and I are sometimes confused about what constitutes a good idea. We both go all in with what feels right in the moment. The time in Los Angeles when I didn't get the job at Hooters and could have exited gracefully, not yelled about the superiority of natural breasts. The time in Madison Square Garden when Devin tried to buy shrooms from undercover cops. The time in San Francisco, the time in Oakland.

August, 1993: Heading for Eugene, Oregon, at five on Friday, we congratulate ourselves on leaving our parents' lives behind. Their weekends are devoted to doctoring a pot roast or pulling a four-foot dandelion root from the backyard; we're blazing a trail to freedom. We consult the map and speculate about the playlist, geek out over the change from California gold to Oregon green.

Saturday afternoon, we're following other Deadheads down a footpath lined with trees and tie dye. For twenty dollars I find an American beauty, sky blue and magenta silk to wrap around my hips or head, to transform the window in our bedroom. At the open market, Dev spots a couple of friendly faces who could be our source for happy bears blotter, so we say hey and sit awhile, work out the deal.

I share my gigantic chocolate chip cookie with the dreadlocked girl whose gold skin wafts patchouli. Dev and his bandannaed new bud hand around the purchase and play hacky sack to a pitchy bootleg from Fillmore West, 1969, their elbows creating visual trails as the girl wraps metallic thread around strands of my long, loose hair. Pleasure ripples across my scalp, down my back, into my fingers. Every fluffy cloud, blade of grass, tree and body is adorned with its own pulsing, iridescent aura. I let go of the feeling that I am an imposter, shake off the eager-to-please nine-to-fiver my bosses pay me to be, and let my head bloom into a rose.

Now, Devin and I have been together for a decade, which surprises us. I watch him mash an anchovy into an egg yolk, squeeze the juice from half a lemon between cupped, slightly fanned fingers to screen out the "pips," whisk it all together with a spoonful of rustic Dijon. Except for a nearly full bottle of bourbon reserved for cooking, there is nothing in the pantry stronger than wine and beer, and our most potent mushroom is shitake.

"How old were you at that Chinese New Year's show? Like ten?" he laughs, tasting, and I marvel that we still act this way, as if it's been nothing but a good old time.

August, 1993: "You're married?" the burnished girl reaches out delicately to touch my hand, the clear, sparkling stone that throws rainbows and matches my nail polish. Soon it will be a year, and still nobody knows, not my folks, not Sue or Frank.

"Me and mine are sharing the ride," she grins, bringing her sleepy baby out of the van, unbuttoning the strap of her hemp top to feed him, skin against skin. She traces circles between his tiny shoulder blades, tanned gold like hers. "Motherhood makes it real," she murmurs. "I had these seizures before he was born, but he got here all right, eight lives to go, so we named him Kitten, sleepy little dreamer in the midnight sun, you know?"

Sometimes I'm not sure I like the Dead, the scene. The music often sounds terrible, the instruments and voices worn-out, and whirling in place while surrounded by thousands of people drunk and on LSD feels unsafe, like navigating a jungle at night. Standing in the endless line for the bathroom is a bizarre kind of torture; women break down in there, in front of the wall of washbasins and endless, warped mirrors.

As if she hears my thoughts, the girl blinks her eyes into the blistering yellow day. "Love is real," she smiles, making a peace sign, and I see that her ring finger is missing.

High on acid the next weekend, I prowl like a cat, stalk the manzanitas on Mount Tamalpais, where we're housesitting for one of Dev's friends. A few days later, riding home on the bus, I realize with certainty that I am pregnant. Dev and I never talk about keeping it. I am afraid that the drugs we take have made us unfit genetic donors, will make us unfit parents, although other people's kids seem to turn out okay.

Now we fight, wage cream puff wars. Our love is precarious, prone to splinter and collapse, more coal than diamond. Each time, we lose a good-sized chunk of that "substance-of-we-feeling" described in my favorite sci-fi novel.

During this round, Dev stands on the deck outside our bedroom, behind our beautifully refinished French doors so that I won't hurl my electric toothbrush at his head. I've been on him about his dad, about why Dev hasn't checked in, and now he's changing the subject.

"What if we've chosen the wrong things for the wrong reasons?" He must mean the baby, the one I didn't want to have, so long ago now. Or maybe he's referring to my business—he often notes how rich it is that parents will trust their children to the childless. I say nothing, hold back the tsunami in my brain. We enjoy acting this way, I think, like characters out of forties' movies, our parents' movies, restrained and almost reasonable until the next cycle of yelling and breaking. I think about a recent dinner with friends, a joke about marriage being the cure for sex, how Devin had laughed and laughed. I stare at the twenty-five pounds he has gained despite cooking with extra-virgin olive oil.

"Every day I feel trapped. The money thing—" he rubs his eyes with strong, agile fingers that have learned to cut onions the way the TV chefs demonstrate, his knife braced against folded knuckles. Dev will never accidentally slice off a fingernail, never carelessly grate blood from a fingertip.

I can't understand why I'm still with him, except I remember. How he is ruled by charisma and tenderness. How I melt at the sight of his dark, hirsute forearms. How he is always willing to share his toys. How when we first met, he was surrounded by a halo of rippling light.

January, 1993: On the morning of the Chinese New Year's show, before we smoke opium, thick and sweet, and float into wedded bliss inside the Oakland Coliseum, we stop for breakfast in the Haight, banana mochas and coconut bars. We discover a new store, new to us at least, named Watch Your Head, located in the basement of a psychedelic t-shirt shop, and we meet our minister-to-be. Hypnotized by shelves of blown-glass pipes with stick-candy twists, I'm not paying attention to Dev and the guy behind the counter, a bearded Jerry lookalike, who are soon deep in conversation.

"*You're gonna give your heart to me,*" Dev calls out, suddenly, sliding his arm around my waist and swinging me in circles between racks of Rastafarian flutes and fanny packs made of indigenous fabric, through swirls of sandalwood incense.

"I'll hook you up," Jerry-guy promises eagerly, "tie your knot, make your sunshine daydreams come true, till death do you part." Devin is all caffeine smiles, and when he shakes Jerry-guy's hand, I see him exchange our cash for something in a baggie. I feel dizzy as we emerge from the candyman's dungeon, and I bump my head on the overhanging stair, try to laugh it off.

Hours later, miraculously—because the Coliseum has turned into a gigantic spaceship with identical sets of airlocks and boarding ramps that materialize at every turn—Jerry-guy reappears. After appraising the crowd, on fire, and the band, smokin' hot, our dude of ceremonies recites passionately from "Sampson and Delilah," waves his magic feather, and pronounces us newlyweds on honeymoon. In the background, the music grows huge and warbles apart like soap bubbles. Chinese dragons exhale kaleidoscopic spirals of smoke as they fishtail through the crowd. Paper confetti drifts onto our hair and eyelashes. When drums send us plummeting into a discordant, throbbing story of how the heart flails and slows and threatens to stop, only to be reignited by love, our two states of consciousness merge, on fire.

Now we keep separate bank accounts. I agree to loan Dev the money, won't give it to him outright. For reasons I don't fully understand, he has started collecting expensive historical artifacts: a totem pole, slave shackles, a powder horn. Maybe he wants to impress the twenty-something art instructor, hired last summer, who has time to play after school. Maybe he knows I think about removing my ring twice a day when children are being dropped off and picked up by so many newly single dads. I haven't officially agreed to the open relationship idea, but here we are.

The night that Sue calls, Dev has just found, online, a punchbowl from the War of Independence and between grading papers is feverishly trying to verify its authenticity. I'm ordering three months' worth of nut-free and gluten-free cookie bars and rice milk boxes for the allergic children of plastic addicts.

"It's Dad," Dev says. When I ask the usual questions, he doesn't answer. He doesn't go right over to the parents' house, and during the week, Frank doesn't let himself in through the garage door to pop up in our kitchen the way he used to, enjoying our surprise every time.

Just a few weeks later, on the date set for the festivus, as Dev insists on calling it, Sue texts to say that Frank can't travel, no way, no how. We re-shelve the good China, pack the rolling cooler, arrive late. Scrambling, we fan out newspaper and distribute Devin's garlicky crustaceans, plunk down a bowl of potato salad garnished with fresh dill and pumpkin seeds. Lifting a plastic dome, we say, "Ta-da!" to reveal glossy buttermilk cake, a triumphant Hail Mary pass after the strawberry soufflé, rushed out of the oven, collapsed. Sue tries to find words that will help Dev and me understand the morphine, why everything is moving so fast.

"Look, Dad's got crabs," Devin tries, setting a full plate on Frank's lap, but the old man is plain out of it, inhaling concentrated O_2 through two pipettes, one in each nostril. He is tiny in the recliner, his knees so thin and wobbly that the orange claws threaten to clatter across the kitchen linoleum.

June, 1978: When Sue first meets Frank in middle age, she sweeps the papers off her courthouse desk and climbs up in their place, arches her back like a diva and entwines her legs, thigh to ankle. She feels her pantsuit pulling tight in all the right places, lets loose an undulating laugh that sets her copious convexities in motion. She wants him that badly, his cheekbones, devilish accent, animal magnetism.

Now, when Sue and I have a chance to talk, she unburdens herself. She doesn't want to blame Frank for getting sick. He joins Alcoholics Anonymous as a sixtieth birthday present to himself and his son, a remarkable turnaround, yet he never kicks the other habits. He rails against demon tobacco despite the crumpled menthol packs that turn up in the trash. When Drive-a-Senior releases him from his volunteer commitment, he denies ever sinking his fingers into the soft flesh of female passengers. He always knows a guy, and before the oxygen tank makes sneaking a toke impossible, he frequently goes out back to "clean the pool" even after it is drained and tarped. Then there is his anger problem.

"When will you let me take the goddamn car to get a goddamn burger?" he wants to know, at three in the morning.

"When you can change your own goddamn Depends," Sue retorts.

She shares this information with a cheerfulness I know conceals despair and vulnerability, the same kind of disguise Devin puts on. I imagine her waiting until Frank falls asleep before reproaching him for dying, for leaving her alone.

It gets real a couple of weeks after Dev's dinner, when Sue invites family members and friends to say their goodbyes. Rarely seen brothers and sisters, their grown children and spouses, descend like proverbial locusts hungry for news, the past, lunch. Bodies overrun the property, but no one thinks to bring food, so Sue orders pizza, runs out for hot wings, Krispy Kremes.

These oily rounds of dough spur Devin into homemade mode. He retrieves his Williams-Sonoma waffle wonder and starts cranking out a variety of flavors—bacon-laden, cream cheese-stuffed, blueberry-dotted—so that the atmosphere turns almost celebratory. Frank even rouses from oblivion to ask if the IHOP waitress has brought two coffees for his sugar.

May, 1995: In Las Vegas, at one of the last shows before Jerry Garcia dies, another chunk of our substance-of-we breaks off. The Dave Matthews Band opens, and the crowd is soon half-naked in the acute heat of the desert, praying for a sun shower, ecstatic with joy when arcs of water fall upon us from hoses wielded by friendly officers. Faces are beatifically transported by music and drugs, by the combined energy of so many gathered solely to share good vibes in a concrete bowl under infinite skies. We are all enjoying the ride, but we are not watching our heads.

By the time night falls, we are sunburned, depleted. In the humid parking structure that reeks of skunkweed and sweat, too many Deadheads are coming down at the same time, one aggregate obstacle to finding our respective cars and getting back to our air-conditioned hotel rooms. Dev needs reeling in, so I feed him the food we packed for that purpose, his naan burritos with dahl and tabouli, my cut-up raw vegetables. As we roam the lot, searching for our car, he eats quickly, reviews every song. I have a question about Delia D. in "Stagger Lee," and he starts to answer, chokes, spirals into the arms of a bad trip.

"I aspirated into my lung," he wheezes.

"Is that even a thing?" Somehow, this will be my fault.

"We have to go to the hospital." He can barely get the words out. Agonized growls punctuate his attempts to regurgitate half-chewed shards he is convinced are embedded in his tissue. He keeps pounding his chest, making gagging noises, and I rub his arm, tell him it's going to be okay. He barks like an actual seal, loudly and violently. I am becoming alarmed.

"I'm pretty sure I tore my esophagus." Sweat breaks out on his nose and forehead.

We've been through this before: apparitions of giant ants, of wounded, weeping trees, how he says my face changes, that I have two faces. I'm having a hard time picturing us under the stabbing lights of an emergency room, explaining his condition to not-tripping nurses and doctors. In desperation, I steer us into the chronic lyricosis game.

"Well, *something something Scarlet Begonias…*Dev?"

"I might be dying. I really might be."

"Come on, how's it start? *Ralph was talkin' 'bout government squared…*"

We've been wandering for a while, and now it's down to us and the most disturbed-looking sleepwalkers who are gaping, needily, from the shadows.

"Dev, I know you know *I'm attuned to the window but not to the air…*"

"Doesn't matter, I'm dying, I feel it."

"Feelings change. *From the other direction, she was combing her lies,* right?"

"Gives me Indian illusion, but...no. NoNoNoNoNo."

"But—I might as well try..."

"Might as well try—" Shouting hoarsely, he falls into a new coughing fit that produces something definitive, something pinkish. The fear begins to slip off my back like rain.

"Now," I instruct, "do it again. Spit into my hand this time."

"Why can't you talk sexy when I'm not dying?"

"I mean it, Devin." He complies. "See? All carrot, no lung."

But the next day, and then for weeks, he complains to our friends that I tried to murder him. He likes to end the story by saying, "'*See?*' All cunt, no heart."

What if he had been about to die? How could he have married such an unkind woman?

Now, because Frank is cremated, there is no closure for us: no drunken, brawling wake, no slideshow and dabbing of eyes, no guilt-ridden gathering of the people who didn't visit in time. So what happens next can be explained, perhaps, in light of our shared grief, in light of our disbelief that Frank is gone little more than two months after we first get the call, in light of Devin's and my hallucinogenic past.

I know I am dreaming—are we all dreaming, collectively?—because afterward, Frank is still dead. But it's one of those extra-vivid visions, a lucid dream, the kind that, when I awaken, makes me question what is real. Am I waking from the dream, or is my day-to-day life the dream? That same sweet song.

Afterward, I know Frank is still dead because Sue has a guy from the program do the things Frank used to do, mow the lawn and pull up monster dandelions. Beside the pool, the ceramic mug that used to serve as an ashtray is clean again and filled with water for stray kittens. But in my dream, my vision, Devin and I head over to the parents' house for early dinner after Frank's cremation. This is meant to be a tribute of sorts, so Dev prepares all the favorites, a Cobb salad with smoked chicken, corn bread and jalapeño compound butter, minted sweet tea, caramel-apple cheesecake.

We turn the corner and let ourselves in the gated backyard, then stop, stunned. There he is—Frank, the dead man—white-toothed and chiseled, sturdier than before.

"We needed room," Sue calls out, waving us over. "All those relations were crowding us!" Frank smiles, but it is the smile of a man who doesn't feel things deeply anymore, who is turning into those things. I want to know if he had a moment of recognition before he left us for good, and is this it.

I look at Dev to see if he has changed, too, if his ripple of light is back, but he is just him, his handsome face and gullible heart. He demands my attention, about to lay down something deep:

"How can you tell the difference between here and gone?"

I want the dream to go in a different direction, now, to show me the other things Devin knows, the funny, shiny things. How when he comes home to find me sitting with the last child of the day, waiting for their mom or dad, he pours us each a cup of juice and pretends to empty his portion into his ear while making silly glug-glug sounds.

"If you're dreaming, you must be here," Dev schools me, pleased. This does have the ring of stoner wisdom, but I watch as our final substance-of-we chunk crumbles away. I remember but can't feel our love. I am stung by its absence, feel the physical ache where I used to feel whole, but now that I see Dev as deficient and foolish, I'm not sure I can stop seeing him that way.

In my peripheral vision, I glimpse a baby—a dream baby, must be— headed straight for the parents' blue tarp that sags precariously over their empty pool. Automatically, as I do every day for the children in my care, I scoop him up, stop him from going astray, and wrap my arms tightly around his hot, squirming body. I want to ask Devin if he's seeing this, too, when Sue announces, "Time to eat, kiddos," so we all move to a table beside a palm tree. Under Frank's direction, we bow our heads.

I'm still holding the baby, trying to feel grateful for whatever it is I'm about to receive.

STARLING

IT WAS THE bees she'd been worrying about, lately, and the bats. There were two syndromes, the one that caused bee colonies to collapse, and the other, where bats' noses turned white as if dipped in powdered sugar, and then they died. She'd also read about the Chilean salmon, unfuzzy creatures, and their infectious anemia, how stressed-out they were from swimming fin upon fin in pens that were too close together. There was Claudia's month-long absence from the Aftermint, and Jake, who was home again but not really there. She was catastrophizing, Jake said so, but everything piled up in her mind. There was the ongoing expense of her bad teeth.

On Monday her dentist had found in Rosie's mouth four new cavities, and all she could think was, those goddamn braces. She wrote a page to her daughter, part of a diary she hoped Star would want to read one day: *If you're thinking about asking your father for braces—the dentist will agree this is a good idea. Not for your self-image, your improved bite and smile, your future in pictures. Because, instead, braces are food traps, and you will not want to floss, you will emerge after four years of retainers and brackets and new, tight rubber bands with straightened teeth full of cavities, and you will have been good for business. This holds true*

*for other improvements to hair and skin, additions and reductions of body
mass—those who supply such treatments will endorse them wholeheartedly,
not for the sake of your health and well-being but for their own.*

Rosie had always prized the name Star. She had danced as Starling
since the beginning, had named her daughter Star as a gift of good
luck. She heard the deejay announce her stage name, and tonight it
worked its old magic: she felt decorated in rays of sunshine, star bright.
She placed the notebook in her locker and headed out to greet the
customers, was surprised to see Peaches on the side stage. Then she
remembered—today was the cocktail waitress's birthday, and Peaches
wouldn't want to miss out on the extra tips.

Backstage, when Rosie had searched for details about the bees and
the bats, she had also typed in "starling," curious about the bird she had
chosen to represent her, based solely on the shimmering image it had
conjured in her eighteen-year-old mind. She was disappointed to learn
that starlings were considered pests, invasives. They were omnivorous,
however, and able to thrive in densely populated urban environments, and
she thought these last qualities might be good omens for her and Star.

When Rosie finished her three songs, Peaches was still swinging
wildly in the trapeze; beneath the waitress, money littered the stage in
piles like raked leaves. Peaches's lips seemed too big for her face and
too wet, and her eyes had pulled back into unconscious slits so that
she barely resembled herself. From this angle, her baby fat pushed out
in a sensual, grabbable way, but Rosie could imagine all that dimpled
goodness sticking around for years, billowing about her waist and
eventually draping like dough from her arms and thighs. This view
of her co-worker stuck in Rosie's mind, competing meanly with the
bubbly, blameless face Peaches used to serve drinks, yet backing up
Peaches's dressing-room revelations of impromptu encounters with all
kinds of men, each less trustworthy than the last.

Just that afternoon, Peaches had bragged (lied?) that her heavily
tattooed boyfriend—of about one week—had taken her drunk
skydiving. Rosie liked the Peaches who dressed like a St. Pauli's girl,
who spoke in a raspy, warm voice when she handed the girls their

Cokes and lime and said, "Looking hot, mama." Rosie could talk to that Peaches.

After Rosie made the rounds and gathered up her own tips, she slipped behind the curtain and down the hall to the locker room, sure the other girls saw her turn her back on the birthday celebration. Between dances, she liked to steal a few minutes alone, presumably touching up her make-up, but instead writing to Star. She tried not to see this as a waste of time.

From the moment Rosie pretended to breeze through the Mint's front door in sunglasses, civilian sundress, and flip-flops until her final, topless grind in full make-up, her time belonged to them—the management, the customers. Her first few hours were reserved for earning the house rent, so there was little reason to exit the building (waste time) while on-shift. In the bar light and pleading music, she always felt a little lost; the men could cleanse their visual palates on silent sports-television and glance with renewed interest at the stage, but she had to continuously play her part, cater to her regulars who expected her to be the same girl every night.

She could try to see things differently. For example, it could be said that her customers had indirectly paid for—were still paying for—her dental work. Devotees had bought her first breast augmentation at nineteen and her second at twenty-one, upgrading her with the best technology at the time: small valves in her armpits through which her cup size could be increased, with her doctor's assistance. At first these gifts had been exciting, but eventually the men became nuisances, good for inexpensive jewelry and pricey chocolates on holidays yet inevitably pitiable when they begged to become her boyfriends. She was married—see?—her diamond ring flashed in the strobe light—to Jake Nemerov, who had deployed three times in the last four years and was still set on reenlisting. She even showed her customers pictures of five-year-old Star, nose-to-nose with her pink and white rat, Shutup. But with Star's toys and clothes, daycare and evening babysitting, Rosie's dry cleaning, and take-out— there was never time to cook—money was always an issue. She had talked to her boss, who set her up on dates with wealthy non-regulars, and these kept the bills paid. She was usually home by two in the morning, four the latest, and Jake might still be on his computer (watching porn?) in the upstairs office, and he'd come to bed after she'd fallen asleep.

Before they were married, she and Jake used to talk. In those early days, he used to tell her stories when she came over to his little apartment. She became the quiet one, listening, or putting an expression on her face that made it seem she was listening while in fact her thoughts wandered out of the room. He was twenty-two and three years a military mechanic, fixing helicopters and thinking he'd like to fly jets out of the middle of the ocean, thinking eventually he'd like to get stationed somewhere like Sicily. After talking about the trouble he had gotten into as a kid, huffing gasoline and setting fire to abandoned houses, together they watched his Britney Spears videos, and she would see herself, even then, as his sexual accessory.

She kept thinking that all the fire in him, all the fuel, would eventually light something in her. One customer had told her she revved like a racecar, and Jake's eyes could burn through her with their Russian cool, but their first time together they moved gracelessly, as though covered in plastic. It got somewhat better after that. When he asked why she had so much lingerie, she was embarrassed to tell him the truth and said the first thing that came into her head: at the tennis club where she had worked, on top of the self-wash machines, the guests left behind new undergarments that had fallen by accident upon the damp concrete floor. And for a while, he believed her. Star was conceived in the first months after they'd met.

Rosie's happiest moments were right before the club opened, putting on makeup with the other girls in the Mint's dressing room. She had learned so much from these women, and their intimacy was contagious; even the lipstick imprints on the mirrors felt like home. There were some she wasn't sure about, like Avalon, a competitive

Marine wife who flaunted her cadre of regulars. Avalon led the clique of tall, flat-chested almost-models, the powerpuffers. Unremarkable or even peculiar-looking in daylight, these girls transformed into glittery, caramel-scented vixens. On the floor they were courted by younger men, stockbroker types, who also played hard to get. Rosie admired these girls, their dispassionate self-confidence, their fussy choice of client, as she wrung an older, drunk "gentleman" out of his suit pants and paycheck, dollar bill by dollar bill, during an hour of steady, sweaty work on a back couch.

Whenever Rosie returned a limp customer to the main stage, she got an appraising once-over from Peaches. Peaches laughed knowingly with the customers, and sometimes Rosie thought about having a drink or two and then, a little drunk, asking Peaches what she really thought—about Avalon's self-importance, about why someone like Claudia had come to the club—about all of them. Maybe even about Star, because Peaches might know something Rosie didn't. It was harder than Rosie wanted, being a mother. Star at five was not Star before being born, when she belonged entirely to Rosie, when Rosie knew everything about her and loved her effortlessly. Star at five was separate and strange, with eyes that looked into her mother and saw her in pieces. If some pieces didn't know how to communicate with other pieces, how could she ever know the right things to say to her daughter?

Her thoughts drifted out of the club and into Star's room, where everything sparkled in pink and purple. Shutup's cage fit neatly into a corner and was likely empty—Jake let him roam the apartment until someone, usually Rosie, thought to put him back. It was sad, having a rat as a pet. Shutup would probably live only a few years before he succumbed to kidney disease or tumorous cancer. Jake had bought the rat for Star so that, he claimed, she could learn to care for a fellow creature, but mainly to placate her when Star's little friend next door had gotten one first. He had named the pet with sarcasm, for his own amusement, and he cracked up every time Star spoke to the animal, her voice almost inaudible. He liked to nudge Rosie in the ribs and ask in a low, satisfied voice, "Worked well, didn't it?"

"What are you doing," Avalon chewed gum near Rosie's ear.

"Nothing really. Just thinking," Rosie turned around in the chair, closed the diary, and stared blankly at the powdered, poreless surfaces of her friend. Were they friends? She certainly preferred it that way.

Avalon put her hand out as if to touch Rosie's chest; instead, her long fingers untwisted Rosie's bra strap. "I was thinking, if I ever got mine done, I'd get them huge. If you pumped yours all the way, you'd easily make bank every night."

Rosie didn't answer. She felt uncertain about her surgeries and their effect upon Star. She felt an urgency to explain herself to her daughter as daily she watched the child move from under her shadow, like a plant reaching for a spot of sun. Sometimes the embellishments she had made to her flesh—supplemented breasts, inflated lips, veneers over her teeth, all intended as improvements—instead made her feel reduced, lowered her body's overall organic-to-manmade ratio. Rosie let her hair fall across her face and searched noisily in her cosmetic bag, emerged with an old nail file. Keeping her head bent, she sawed at the tips of her fingers. Avalon sat down across from her in front of the makeup mirror and reapplied purplish metallic lipstick.

"You shouldn't do that, you know," Avalon said to Rosie's reflection, "back and forth like that. Only file in one direction."

Rosie thought of the night she and Claudia teamed up and told Avalon to call the customers "sycophants" when they annoyed her. Avalon thought the word meant "sicko" but said it anyway and did well in chagrin-induced tips.

"Poor fish," Claudia had said; Rosie hadn't asked which of them, customer or dancer, was the fish. She thought again of the Chilean salmon, the bees, the bats, the closeness and claustrophobia of the club, the insecticide sprayed on the walls and floors after the girls went home, the rat race her customers returned to after spending their nights with her. Rosie missed Claudia, the way she had danced to '80s rock ballads with her eyes closed, the long brunette fall clipped into her bobbed hair, her skirted bikini imprinted with smiling stick-figure girls in crayon colors. Rosie had never seen Claudia move in a manner that could be considered lewd.

"When is your husband going back?" Avalon buzzed in Rosie's ear.

Rosie lied, "He's not. He's home to stay this time." Sometimes it seemed that men like Jake were waiting for war, almost lonesome after it. The time between wars existed only to be filled with women, and with giving them children—proof of sacrifice, duty, valor, potency.

"There's a play," Avalon went on, "that Peaches told me about? Where all the women of the town or whatever refuse to have sex with their husbands until the men stop having their war. Women so rule, you know?"

The deejay called out, "Starling!" Rosie bent at the waist and checked the mirror to make sure no safety pins were showing; two ovals of glitter, small as the palms of her hands, had fallen or rubbed off the back of her shorts. Avalon followed her, still chatting. Moving to the music in her usual too-fast fashion, Rosie tried hard to enjoy herself, but all she could see was Avalon at her stage, laughing, and Peaches too, standing with her drink tray resting on one raised knee. Their mouths were open, showing little pointed teeth, hyper-white in the darkened room.

Rosie's head flooded so full, she could barely manage on her three-inch heels. She leaned into the pole and prayed not to fall. *Star, although I know it is too late, I cannot be the mother you most need. Please do what your father asks, but know your own mind. If, when you are older, you believe that obtaining some object or person will give your life purpose, push that thing away. The manmade things, the outside things, will never...* She forced her attention back to the audience.

When Rosie first knew she was pregnant with Star, she didn't tell Jake. Their relationship was not defined; he wouldn't call for days, and neither would she, holding ground. Then he would phone late at night, inviting her over for what turned out to be rambling conversation strewn with bits of the kind of sex he required. She couldn't say if she wanted a child, but in her head she heard clearly: *You cannot kill your baby.* She never thought to ask, instead: *How will I care for this life?*

The time before last, Jake came home with two deep scars, still raw-looking: bad burns across the back of his right hand and down the top of his thigh, to his knee. When Rosie asked what had happened, he didn't answer. He had an inch of blonde, fuzzy hair on his head, standing straight up, so sweet and vulnerable.

"Let's go shopping, babe, for you and Star. Whatever you want, we'll get it," his usual way of putting her off. Instead of driving to the Marine Corps Exchange, he took her to a department store and bought real silverware—a delicate, precious set. While passing the new skillets and casseroles, he sighed and confessed. "Look, we were drinking, letting off steam. I was frying up potatoes, it was a goof—the pan dumped. I caught fire..." She could see him then, what must have really happened, his nose flaked with white powder, an unclothed woman screaming or laughing and calling an ambulance.

Then he wouldn't go out in the sun. He wouldn't make love and instead soothed himself with the internet. They started the habit of eating outside at dusk, with the new silverware, at the picnic table in their complex's tiny courtyard. The scrape of silver against their cheap Corelle plates suggested to Rosie their compromise: his war for this peace, for these brief evenings of hope and last light, exactly what Jake said he must fight to uphold. But what holds us, Rosie wanted to know, staring into her husband's dark sunglasses.

The next time, Jake might come back without his hands, his legs. His body might be embedded with shrapnel. He might not come back at all. If she could just hand Star over to Peaches, or better yet, to Claudia… Claudia must be a good mother. Claudia surely sang songs in Spanish to her own daughters, told them stories that ended happily. Rosie could imagine Claudia standing in a warm kitchen and wearing her smiling bikini, slicing lemons into a pitcher of iced tea, dancing with her daughters, dancing with Star. Claudia would clean the knife and put it away, sway her hips playfully to let the girls know just how much they were loved. Claudia wouldn't write a letter to her daughter that started out by saying: *After the war, everything was parts*. After Claudia disappeared, though, there had been a note taped to the inside of her locker, a note Rosie had saved. It was handwritten, and the print was smudged, and it said, "Let *him* wonder where *you* have been all night."

When the last of her songs faded out, Rosie bent quickly to scoop her tips and clothes off the floor, trying not to appear awkward. She refused to scoot around on all fours the way the newer girls did. A sudden volley of bills, crumpled into tight biscuits and aimed at the exposed parts of her anatomy, confused and slowed her exit as the next showgirl brushed past. Rosie saw Avalon and Peaches, still laughing at the foot of her stage, throwing paper bullets fed to them by the men upon whose laps they wriggled.

As if to keep her from escaping, the cozy group switched to a battle rap: *Starling, darling, it's alarming—heard your Snack Pack's stale like Cracker Jack, wants its sexy back, darling. Heard your salt lick tastes like garlic, must be karmic, darling.*

Rosie felt her poise give way, then her legs. She sat inelegantly, one arm held tightly against her exposed breasts, both hands clutching her money. She could tell she had broken a nail.

One night during her first weeks with Jake, when he would talk and talk her into a dizzying state of inertia so that all she could do was plead silently for him to touch her, she'd broken out of her trance. She'd straddled him, worked a few dollars into his jeans front pocket, and teased, mimicking the persistent men from the club, "No more talking—let's get rocking!"

He hadn't liked that. He'd taken her money and put it in the garbage, his eyes like ashes. They'd argued, and she'd told him the truth, most of it, about her job at the Mint. When they finally had sex, as many times as they could manage, it was almost morning. Birdsong trembled behind the windows, and Rosie saw and felt Jake for the first time.

On the stage that was no longer hers, where the next girl was already half-naked and throwing looks, Rosie felt exhausted. She closed her eyes and thought she'd call Jake to get her, just this once. She saw herself lying beside him in bed, her body beginning to lift up, released, as he talked to her the way he used to. It was almost midnight, and she guessed he was at his computer, Star flung across the covers of her pink and purple bed, lost in sleep, Shutup not yet back in his cage. She would call her husband and make herself soft, inviting, just to hear his voice, whatever part of him was available.

She walked toward the dressing room, rehearsed her words. "Hey—it's me, surprise." Or: "Jake—I know this sounds crazy, but—the fuzzy creatures—we're going to be okay, aren't we?" Her fingers hovered over the keypad. They were innocent babies, all of them.

HO-DADDY

ANGUS ADMITTED to being a punk and a slut, a user while in his teens.

"I like that you used to be a bad boy," I prodded. We were watching the movie *Rush*, where undercover narcotics cops get hooked on the drugs they purchase.

"Don't like it too much," Angus said.

His words sounded familiar, and I should have recognized them as Officer Jim Raynor's, but I didn't.

"So…if we found some drugs, like under that wiggly floorboard" (it seemed obvious that this was where the previous tenants had stored their stash), "there's no way you'd do them with me?" I asked this despite what he had told me when we first met: that having a "chippie," even a part-time habit, was a deal-breaker.

Angus said, "I don't think you'd like me on drugs. I act like dog food," which only intrigued me further. I didn't believe him, that he would treat me badly. I had formed deep bonds while intoxicated and remembered sex under the influence as some of the best, like riding waves in tandem. When he said he used to be a ho-daddy, I started to sweat, thinking I had found a real surfer, but he clarified this meant he'd hung out on the shore and flirted with the girls while his friends waited on their boards for the next big one.

Sweating: I erroneously interpreted this reaction as a sign of fate, that I had no choice but to dive in. Like in the New Age nursery with the beautiful bi-boy who informed me, provocatively, that it took a woman seven years to get a man's *chi* out of her system, who gave me hot flashes whenever I saw him, every couple of months, his *chi* squeezing mine as he wrapped brown butcher paper around some gargoyle I'd bought just to watch him stamp it all over with dolphins. The night he invited me to a party, I made the first move and later couldn't remember how he felt except too big all over. I could picture only his hands, which before the act held a persuasive magic and afterward seemed to float upon his torso like carved bars of soap.

I met Angus just before he got his flipper, three false teeth on a wire that restored his smile to charming. I was working part-time at the front desk of a dental office until I finished hygienist school, moving through my routine as through neck-high water, sometimes catching myself staring, mesmerized, at my coworkers' hair scrunchies that bobbed like multicolored fish. Between work and classes I drifted, looking for men at the gym, in the clubs, in the museums, at the beach. Angus's mouth was packed with gauze, and his eyes had just returned from anesthesia land, where he'd had several teeth pulled because that was the cheapest option. When I returned his credit card, he gave me a cockeyed smile and two thumbs up, and something hooked into me. In his easy, confident way, he asked for my number, and I gave it to him because everyone deserved a chance.

That weekend we rode the bus together to a hill in a park I hadn't been to before, rolled out a blanket and listened to a free concert. I brought Tupperware filled with raspberries that he poked at, recoiling from the red stain on his fingers as if he had been stung. This seemed weird, but I didn't want to judge. After an hour he told me he couldn't sit on the ground any longer because of his condition, so we packed up and took the bus back to his place.

We were lying side by side on his futon when he said, "I love you," and I heard this as a question that required a response.

"I love you, too," I said. I didn't, yet, but I wanted him to know I saw he was lovable and needed something from me that I could afford, right then, to give.

After *Rush* ended, I mixed tequila and orange liqueur until the pitcher was three-quarters full, squeezed in limes, added ice, and convinced Angus to exchange his beer for a glass or two. Soon we were trying to pry up the loose floorboard.

I knocked on it excitedly. "Hear that? Sounds hollow, right?" and then he knocked, and then we drank some more. But no matter how hard he tried, he couldn't get the board to budge, and after a while the pitcher was empty. The edginess of the movie and the drinking made me want to go out, but dancing wasn't an option for Angus, and I didn't like the local bars. I suggested that we go for a night hike even knowing that his condition made long walks difficult.

Lately he couldn't bear to touch any kind of citrus, but because of the tequila he must have made an exception—he grabbed my hand even though it reeked of limes and pulled me almost roughly onto the broken sidewalk that led to the street. Party music warbled from a row of Mexican fan palms, a blooming cactus garden, the waning moon. I opened my mouth to tell him, and he kissed me so hard I thought we were fighting.

We weaved drunkenly for a few blocks and ended up on a stranger's front porch. Angus rang the doorbell repeatedly, dared me to go inside. I pushed him away and ran. By the time he caught up, I was shaking with adrenaline and the uncool feeling I wore all through high school like body odor or pit stains—the knowledge that, despite my tattoos and piercings, at foundation I was a *no* person. As if he guessed what I was thinking, he laughed and lit a cigarette.

We continued up the road. From that point on, I didn't know why, but I started seeing certain houses as mirages and the people in them as cartoonishly, even dangerously, exposed. Lantern-trimmed balconies, one after another, appeared claustrophobic instead of cozy, and the most elaborate lots, with houses at the top of terraced hillsides, seemed the most vulnerable to, or maybe deserving of, plunder and violence. These houses actively repelled me. The entire hillside was covered with them, and none of them would ever be ours. I clung to Angus's arm so as not to be sucked into the darkness behind other people's curtains, the darkness that sat in armchairs, held shotguns, and waited for the signal from the dogs.

Still, we climbed. When we reached a turn in the road with an undeveloped lot on one side and a construction site on the other, Angus stopped.

"Lie down," he said, and without thinking, I did. His body folded next to mine, and I breathed deeply, tried to relax. Lush scents surrounded us—eucalyptus and night-blooming jasmine, angel's trumpet—but I lay uneasily, cold against the hard concrete, unable to speak to anything. I saw myself in different overlapping circles, the buzzy, drunk place inside my head, the alien neighborhoods that surrounded us, the mysterious habitats of nonhuman things, the unreachable, expanding universe. I didn't see how I could thrive in any of these. The alcohol in my stomach churned and soured.

After a while, the tar roadway, a kind of piecrust over dirt and rock, started to warm and give way toward the deep center, and I imagined we were being held in the palm of a giant hand. Then it became important to choose an exact location: *Which side of the painted line do you want? I like it on the line itself, feels smoother.* We spoke in whispers, and I confessed to Angus that in our city life, I often forgot the sky was full of stars; tonight, they were mirrors. He nodded in agreement.

During our first date, sitting on the hill grimacing at my raspberries, Angus had described his daily physical pain, caused by a high school car accident further complicated by falling off a roof. His spine had been damaged, and the loss of motor control extended into his hands and feet, which randomly cramped and convulsed.

With growing compassion, I listened to his compelling story. Soon,
I accepted his drinking as a substitute for the pharmaceuticals he
had learned to avoid. His allergies were harder to understand, but
I made room for them: after raspberries, he hated loose change,
which he'd throw in the garbage. Whenever I became confused by his
sudden coolness or tentative touch, or when I tired of his shitfaced,
philosophical lectures, I told myself to be patient, that he was a delicate
creature. I made room for his condition, but I remained curious about
the other part of him that had been broken.

Lying on the road, the stillness and the stars and the smell of
flowers met inside me in a way that made me want to relinquish
something, one unneeded thing. I was weary of feeling that I didn't
know what I was doing, of needing magical signs to guide me, of
being disappointed. I tried to make my brain *an unformed unity of
empty cognizance*, a meditation I had read in a Buddhist magazine.
The magazine's cover photo of a famous and handsome actor had
been encouraging, a promise that kind men with good intentions
were, in fact, on the planet, despite much evidence to the contrary.
I was suddenly aware of the sureness of Angus, his slender warmth
offering itself to me.

Our hands reached toward each other, clasped. We lay like that
for a while, my head blank and open, my skin warm where it pressed
into his, arm against arm, leg against leg. The other side of my body
felt cold, immobile. I heard the rumble of an approaching vehicle,
knew that people in our neighborhood took these roads fast, knew
they drove drunk and high and thought they could drive just fine until
they ran into something. The ground throbbed and trembled as the
engine grew louder, our world tipping too fast. Headlights skimmed
our bodies, and my skin stiffened with panic as the machine turned
toward us.

I didn't scream, couldn't get enough air in my lungs, and time
compressed and slowed in the way of dreams. I remembered a visit to
the new age garden shop, my bi-boy who, after our hookup, had shaved

his head into the softest fur. How he let me run my hand over his head, how I fell in love again. The girl who interrupted us, asking for something—he was working, after all—and how angry I felt, reading the embroidery on the back of her leather jacket, *double suicide is the truest form of love*. This memory, this anger, flashed through me in the moment it took the driver to gun the curve.

In the sharp blue glare of the headlights, I held fast to Angus's hand and breathed shallowly as wheels bore down upon us and felt, along with the rush of metal and the alarmed, angry shouts of the driver, a kind of relief, the inevitability of our choice now that it was playing out in the worst way. I would become the splintered bones and spattered blood of the movies we watched. I squeezed Angus's fingers, entwined in mine, to let him know we were in accord, when I felt him go rigid, his wrist and arm locking painfully in a full-on spasm, my hand caught in the impossible strength of his involuntary convulsion.

Pebbles sprayed and stung my face. I inhaled burnt rubber and engine oil. The instinct to leap away vacated my body. I rolled more closely toward Angus, our faces touching, our arms inextricably linked. The rest of him wasn't even trembling. I squeezed my eyes shut and felt his breath against my forehead, his slow smile, his stuck arm an iron lever forcing my *no* switch into the *yes* position.

As the driver swerved around us, I felt something collide with my shoulder, bouncing off too fast to really hurt. The vehicle made a sickening, grating sound against the edge of the asphalt, and I began to cry into Angus's chest. Another object hurtled toward our heads; this one hit the ground, hard, and instantly my hair was soaked. I heard wheels burn around the curve ahead and spin into the distance, and Angus went limp.

We managed to stand upright and move to the embankment, Angus using his good arm as a sling for his swollen, pale hand. My own felt as if it had been crushed in a vise. Walking, sticky with soda from the thrown can, I felt the imprint of the road on our arms and legs, the rush of blood through my head. Cloud cover obscured the stars, the sky darker now, shot through with violet. I could still smell eucalyptus, sharp and earthy, but the jasmine had faded. We began the slow walk home.

"When I was in school," Angus said, "I used to play chicken at the airstrip. I would always take a dare, the more outrageous the better. Totaling cars, girls, I mean, bad shit happened to me too, when I was a little kid, but shit always happens even when you're not looking for it. So I started looking."

I wanted to ask if he had jumped, not fallen, off that roof, the one that broke his back.

He went on, "After what happened to my body, I was done with going along, with pulling stunts just because someone needed a laugh, a scapegoat, a hero. I had played chicken with pain, and pain had won. But pretending that there was no pain crept into everything—I couldn't say what I felt, what I thought—not that anyone cared, anyway."

I waited for him to tell me the last part, the realization part, because I finally understood that his weird allergies were little pieces of bitterness. I wanted him to be done with the bitterness, too, to say something like, "When I saw that my pain wasn't going away, I had to stop treating people carelessly, since that just hurt me worse."

But he didn't say this. Instead, he offered me some line I didn't recognize from some movie I hadn't seen. Cold and tired, I smiled, trying to understand how we made sense. *I am an unformed unity of empty cognizance.*

It was almost morning by the time Angus passed out, but I couldn't sleep. Drawn to that loose floorboard, I turned on my phone flashlight and slid a screwdriver out of the kitchen drawer, careful not to make too much noise. I knelt and fiddled with one edge of the board, surprised when the whole thing pulled up easily. Inside, I found a spy camera positioned beneath a tiny hole drilled through the wood, a hole nobody would notice if they weren't looking for it. Later in the week, I discovered a similar black pinprick on our bathroom mirror, and I learned that the silver paint behind the glass could be scratched off in a way that was barely noticeable. When I confronted Angus, he admitted that both cameras were his.

Because I still loved him, and because it seemed like something I could afford to give, I let him watch me for a few more days. Then I couldn't, anymore.

I completed my hygienist program and found a good job with a dentist who had recently started her own practice. I liked her spa-like décor, her state-of-the-art equipment, and her mouthful of gold fillings, a kind of advertisement. One evening after work, alone, I turned on the television and started watching *The Notebook*, which I had always dismissed as too sappy to be worth my time. But I was still a little raw after Angus, and something sappy felt like just the thing.

Early in the courtship between Noah and Allie, I experienced a moment of recognition followed by mild shock. Angus had used a whole scene on me—the one where Noah lies in the middle of an intersection and challenges Allie to join him. The movie's scene and our experience on the road were too alike to be a coincidence.

I considered how many lines, how many scenes, Angus had passed off as his own. I didn't want to keep thinking about his pain, his continued need for the rush, his ability to disregard what came after. I just wanted his *chi* out of my system.

I pictured him with a new girl, maybe at the beach, on their first date. He wouldn't be able to sit too long because of his condition, and because his latest antipathy was to sand. For a few minutes he might watch the surfers, their perfect, unbroken bodies, their good intentions. Then he would glance at the girl sitting next to him, her shining face, and think: out of all of them, he was definitely the winner.

THE FURNACE

AFTER THE LAST day to cancel their deposit came and went, they were on a plane out of New York, the coastline far behind them, much to Leah's relief. They arrived in Amsterdam at night, in the rain, and made their way, on foot, to the medieval center of the city. The weighty, stable-like doors of their residence were resistant to their key, but these gave way, at last, to a spacious mud room, a galley, and a second-story bedroom with an old-world view. The single bathing room, finished in blue-veined marble and coral stone, was lavishly outfitted with thick, heavy towels, a triple sink that stretched out beneath silver-flocked mirrors, and craned lighting. As they should have expected, the ancient plumbing was a nightmare. Furiously scrubbing the travel-grime from her skin, Leah stood ankle-deep in water that wouldn't recede. She hadn't gone to the salon before they left, and now her curls were halfway down her back, a ragged tangle whose frayed ends broke and drifted like seaweed alongside the other human detritus that swirled ever closer to but never down the drain.

They were sharing, with a Swede and two Australians, a rare find—a four-story firehouse in the Red Light District. Leah and her husband had argued over this without conciliation; she believed everything would be genial overall, their privacy a small price to pay to live in an authentic canal house built in the Dutch Golden Age. Her husband, a pragmatic guardian of his own comforts, retained doubts.

The next morning, her husband took his turn in the trickling, mounting rivers of the shower while the rest of their group breakfasted in the communal kitchen. One by one, coffee unfurled from pods like dark flowers. She made his the way he liked it, nearly black, a lick of milk and teaspoon of sugar that swirled and settled at the bottom of the cup.

The Aussie sisters, Jippa and Willow, were snub-nosed and pretty, as welcoming and sociable as two young dolphins. Jippa spun Spam-and-eggs and biscuits with gravy while Willow stabbed at Moroccan-spiced chicken and red barley from the night before, cold. The Swede, who owned the place, kept stretching his long, restless legs into impossible positions, a yogic tic, perhaps. He'd introduced himself as "a student of life," but Leah decided he was a brute, conscious or unwitting. He ate the eggs with his fingers and made a false show of courtesy each time he stepped outside to smoke his cannabis.

His eyes skimmed over the thick-haired sisters with whom, in his straightforward way, he'd been quick to recommend the city's most popular coffeeshops, but his attention tugged at Leah like an animal that wanted petting. Already she'd caught his stare move across her breasts to her belly. His resemblance to a legendary songwriter known also as a tantric practitioner, combined with the contortionism and smoke fetish, led her to imagine he was deviant in bed, a devotee of surfaces and sensations. This thought aroused and humiliated her.

Light reached them from mullioned, multicolored windows, a different light than came and went in her husband's home—she still thought of it as belonging to him alone—in the South. There, sunlight broke through whorled panes of glass and threw shadows of tree branches across the walls. In the peculiar way of old houses that had been modified over time, four doors now faced each other in the spot where the light consolidated, the spot where the original furnace had lived. It was senseless, she knew, but sometimes, in protest against the house she had not chosen, the house her husband and his ex-wife had furnished and altered to their tastes, Leah closed herself into this four-walled room, a novitiate's cell as wide only as her angled elbows, and sat, knees drawn up, until her body disappeared and she forgot which doors led outward. She thought of this while she waited for her husband to join them.

The Swede—to herself she called him Brutus—dangled one pale, furred leg over the arm of a thin-carved chair, reached into the liquor cabinet and ran his thumb across label after label.

"Why Netherlands? Do you have people here?" He spoke to her as if she were the only one in the room.

Conscious of her husband's absence, she let the words trickle out, at first: he had family here; they traveled infrequently but now were taking advantage of his approaching retirement and diminishing caseload; they were escaping the plantation, hyperbolically named, or simply "the burden" as they referred to his century-old property; they were seeking cooler zones to calm her hot internal climes. Had she said that last part out loud?

She had been here once before on New Year's Eve, her last year at college. She remembered standing knee-deep in colored-paper streamers, the sky pierced and jeweled with fire, how the women in the Red Light District stared at her from behind glass and lewdly proffered triple scoops of flesh. She had been so young, then, able to burn effortlessly through one romantic complication and into the next.

She explained their back-story, how she had left the golden, placid coastline of California for the green and blistered South because of their old love, re-formed. She and her husband had fallen in love— Leah blushed to say it—when they were younger, had returned to their separate lives, had found each other again. She spoke loudly, hoping her husband would hear, would remember to miss her the way he had during the years they were apart, would come downstairs to encircle her in the narcotic of his arms, would reclaim her in front of Brutus and the girls.

"Is he your soulmate, then?" Jippa reached into a clatter of mismatched silverware and handed her sister a spoon that they took turns dipping into the same jar of purple jam. Rain was falling again, the outdoor market in Leiden closed until later in the week, and maybe they wanted a reason to stay inside a while longer until the museums opened. Maybe they enjoyed listening to her vampire story of undying love and could believe, as she did, that her husband had never stopped thinking about her, had spoken her name as if she could be summoned, as if she were the drug that would obliterate his despair. Maybe they wanted to shiver, as she had, with the recklessness of his reaching out to her after what had been almost too many years, then the anguish of leaving his wife and alienating his family, all to bring her back.

Leah went on, even against her better judgment.

Their love had flared dangerously, steadied. They set a date, purchased rings, practiced calling each other husband and wife with real tenderness. She had always loved how he held his depths—maybe it sounded alien to say so, but she felt that his appendages from brain to digit burrowed outward as sensitively as his inward self received. In the beginning, she was at her best when she could, without distraction, tend to him, when her own depths, still mysterious to her, were used for his pleasure. Some nights, her desires colluded to produce suspenseful movie-fantasies she thought her husband would enjoy, and sometimes he did. These gelatin-silver shows nearly consoled them.

The other truth was that their first year together had been unexpectedly hard. More Frankenstein than Vampyre, she almost killed the thing they had brought back to life. That first summer, after her husband left for work, she ran, refusing to succumb to the heat or humidity or absence of air that moved. She pushed herself across ungiving concrete despite deep cracks that appeared in the bottoms of her feet, making it painful to walk. She ran past mildewed fences, past goats, chained and collapsed in half-dirt front yards, past so many dogs, tall as children and with long, human faces, barking worriedly behind wrought iron gates they could easily jump over, her stomach seizing at the thought. She ran past sour, leering trash containers tipped ominously into her path; past the courtyard tombstone of a beloved son, irrevocably deployed; past the neighboring circle of granite that promised a gothic ritual. This circle reminded her of the center of her husband's house where the four doors met, where the absent hearth still conjured a vortex or vanishing point. Each time she ran toward the embrace of stones, sharp grass pushing up in ragged, indefatigable clumps, she felt ugly and small.

Attuned to everything in the house, Brutus said, "I am listening," as he disappeared into his room and returned wearing a silk robe and boxing trunks. He sat on the floor, lotus-style, stretched and wrapped his arms around his body, massaged the silken glint on his forearms and thighs. "I am listening, yes." In her mind's movie, in an image so abruptly clear it felt as if Brutus had placed it there, he lay with her on her husband's bed as she arched and lowered her body, her husband gripping some article, perhaps a belt, uncoiled against his own naked hip.

She heard a soft groaning upstairs and paused—the tap at last closed?—then a new thrumming, a different keen of water tumbling into one of three sinks. Waves of heat pitched from her waist to her head. Sometimes she saw herself as unable to turn away from whoever might want her, the way every mirror in her husband's house produced a different likeness, and she could not resist looking back with fascination, sometimes horror, at each new person.

She frowned at her husband's cup of coffee, grown cold, and said that the flight to Amsterdam had felt like a warning. At take-off, as they gathered speed, their bodies were suddenly thrown forward. The plane shuddered to a stop then sat inert on the runway for an hour, everyone in shock. At last, they were allowed to disembark.

They drank their dinner in a bistro with a view of the tarmac while mechanics in orange jumpsuits made repairs. After a few hours, almost all reboarded the same plane, unbelieving even as they re-stashed their carry-ons. Once they reached cruising altitude, some made jokes about the Donner Party, the Titanic, the Hindenburg. A resourceful attendant gathered up the children and kept them busy handing out peanuts and crackers, cold, palm-sized apples. One cherub hovered by their seats, and she and her husband exchanged a look to say they could imagine the child as their own. She wanted to give the girl a gift, remembered

she had just the thing in her change purse, a button shaped like a
flower. Perfect for a little jean jacket or daypack, it had hot pink petals
with a bright orange center, but at the last second, she was unable to
hand it over, her heart thudding and her forehead beaded with sweat.

Throughout the remainder of the flight, she sat as if drugged.
The effort of choosing a movie or TV show seemed too great, or too
inconsequential, so she watched the other passengers' screens from
behind their backs. Just before landing, seat trays and limbs began to
rattle and jerk violently. A woman jolted awake and began to cry at the
man beside her, "You are never how I need you!" Forcing up the shade,
Leah saw the plane nose into blindness, pull up with urgency, and
begin a terrifying circle in endless fog.

Her husband slept through everything—when they were forced
to land in a city whose name she didn't know, when the plane guzzled
fuel, when several passengers clamored to disembark for a rumored bus
but soon returned and re-belted, avoiding each other's eyes. He slept
even as they again rose and fell under clouds that had lifted sufficiently
to let them bounce and swerve to their original destination. She had to
awaken him with two hands, murmured caresses from her throat, her
fingers running lightly over the ridges of his ears until his twilight brain
reached the surface, ascended into light. Eyes still closed, he repeated
the three syllables of his ex-wife's name like a mantra, and Leah resisted
the desire to scream.

She went to the sink and filled her cup with water, drank thirstily.
She felt dehydrated and jet-lagged and wasn't sure where she had left off.

"How terrible, the flight! Please go on," Willow said.

Now that she and her husband were together again, Leah explained
that she felt almost victimized by her love for him. Her body was newly
receptive to the slightest invasions, pleasant and unpleasant. True, she
experienced an abrupt end to the suffering of longing. But in its place,
she gained an awareness of moving past mirrors that reflected someone
else's skin, as she had told them earlier. She believed that even as she
pressed her face against her husband's body and made his scent familiar,
as she touched and pulled from him the fine wavelengths that radiated

as he slept, still he receded and embedded more deeply into himself. She began to see human behavior in tableaus of men's and women's separate pain, even as she protested this was how her ancestors lived. Alone in the kitchen, preparing dinner before her husband returned from work, she feared the subjugation would go on forever: the hearts of men would continue to swell dangerously as they discussed themselves; the women would weep over dull knives yet manage to slice their blood into everything.

These thoughts pierced and tortured her as she lay beside her husband at night. Now that they were reunited, now that the agony of separation was alleviated, she ached for coalescence. She wanted each to be captive to the other, bound by physical ties if necessary, each magnetized to the other's needs. She wanted to be his jagged blood cells and contracting muscles and even the nerves that inflamed and immobilized him, their brains touching and lips parted, gulping air, in union. She didn't understand the origin of this need, just its disturbing force, and she shouldn't have said out loud that this was the foundation of her love that had held, even strengthened, during their twenty years of silence and ignorance of the destructive, self-flagellating arcs of each other's lives.

She paused here to look at Brutus, who was rolling a slim, frosted bottle between his palms with the same concentration he displayed while flexing his torso. When she studied these men—her husband sidestepping the accretion of perfumed, soapy hair but neglecting to throw it away after he left the shower, Brutus extending his legs as if preening around a tail, both oblivious to anything but the sensations of their own bodies—she felt jealousy. She was certain they abandoned themselves to their pleasures, including their belief in the compelling weakness of the feminine. This was one reason for preserving their old, dimly lit edifices—such homes asserted their attraction to the structures of the past and proclaimed they didn't want to see. She, on the other hand, needed her suicide mirror, had to know exactly where the money, shotgun, cemetery plot was and who else was buried in it. Meanwhile, these men knew how to turn their fingers to barometers of marble-smooth and liquid, could make their lovers feel, for a time, like the flawless, blameless center of everything. In the end, they took what they wanted without apology. She was tired of being susceptible to these manipulations.

Was she still speaking? Her husband had not yet made his way down the narrow, carpeted stairs. The girls had gone out despite the rain. Brutus stood, grabbed the edge of the table, and dropped his knee to the floor in a lunging motion. His breath was a solid substance, rippling beneath the continuous organ of his skin. He was ridiculous, but so was she. She thought again of him as an animal, entering her, and she shuddered at how he would feel.

"I think," she said at last, "that we might be haunted."

In her husband's house, in the four-doored cell where the furnace had once burned its coals to oily ash, she sometimes saw a ghost-vision, a movie-man so distinct he seemed more than a product of her mind alone. She watched as this apparition chose a wife, then another. Custom compelled him, or fate—an ancient thread hovered outside his perception and worked itself through him, commandeered him with a practiced hand.

Leah watched it all from her seated position in the cloistered chamber, her eyes closed but seeing, the movie playing out in flickering shadows upon colorless wood. She saw the delicately inked love letters that First Wife set on fire when Second Wife, no more than a concubine, entered the house. When Third Wife moved her belongings into the marital bedroom, Leah watched First Wife unfasten her heavy necklaces, release from her hair a dark red stone on a golden wire, twist off her rings, and thrust each of these through the hot metal mouth of the furnace. When First Wife knelt and placed a differently shaped bundle upon the flames, Leah did not open her eyes.

There were no children until Third Wife. Then Leah saw how the house came alive with happiness, Third Wife young enough to be First Wife's daughter. In time, however, the thread gathered knots: Second Wife, bound to her opioid illusions, poisoned her mind. Third Wife was caught and held between two carriages while she stood in the middle of the street, exchanging pleasantries with a shopkeeper. As if in compensation for so much loss, First Wife and her husband were returned to one another. He had loved the others, but his thoughts always flew to her, and although their youthful delirium was a memory, he still found her beautiful.

One evening while he bathed, a ruby rolled out of the fire and would not stop burning, telling the story of First Wife's secrets. Soon he would understand how she had destroyed his letters, his gifts of jewelry, and most cruelly, for he hadn't known it existed, their unborn child. Leah watched as First Wife climbed into the furnace.

Leah, too, had done something similar, once she saw that the man who was now her husband would not leave his wife. She had unceremoniously dumped in the trash the love letters she was keeping for them both. She had then leapt into the furnace of forgetting, never saying no to an opportunity for love.

Brutus held out his hand.

On the first evening after she and her husband met again, changed the course of their lives for each other, she wept for hours, knowing she was a thief. Now some nights she grabbed him, bit until she tasted blood, dug her nails into the palms of his hands, into the sensitive flesh of his neck, never getting to the heart of him.

"Come on," Brutus laughed, pulling her into his soft fur. "Yes? *Gezellig en warm*, the Dutch way." Her head began to hum, on high alert: the doors of the firehouse were difficult to open, especially with the rain; the girls would knock and knock, but no one would let them in.

Brutus held her more tightly against the thrilling animal warmth of his chest until a sound came out of her throat, a shard of laughter that felt like failure. She saw, as if she were looking down from the top of the stairs, two entwined shadows, each laughing for a different reason. Neither saw what was funny about their embrace, how something would be destroyed, probably her.

BLISS

FOR COREY, the game had changed. Not just the new, online role-playing game he was totally into, *Monsters vs. Heroes,* which made his heart thrill with the beauty of its flying mounts, its borderless landscapes, its reeling cacophony of quests, but the real thing, the three musketeers' one-for-all brotherhood had reached its endgame, zenith, whatever. He was losing his best friend, Jason, had lost him already to this usurper, this Jenna, this fried-franchise princess, and he knew how that made him sound: like a pussy when he wasn't.

He heard his father's voice even when he willed himself not to, always that rising, falling gavel-song of caution against the "libturds" and what they liked to do, that calloused, incongruously smooth-nailed hand reaching out to demonstrate…and then, always, a blackness that left him feeling sick. But there was no shame in his love for Jason, his real love for his best friend. It wasn't like he was *in love* with Jason; he knew himself enough to know that. Still, he couldn't explain why he felt like crying, real salt, and had to force a smile when Jason told him and A.J. the news, man-to-man-to-man, just the three of them over beers at Jason's apartment.

"I'm marrying her, dudes. I'm gonna manage a couple of their

Vegas KFCs, we're gonna live the life." Jason raised his beer in the three musketeers' salute.

Corey's smile held, but his large hand trembled and knocked the neck of his Newcastle painfully against his front teeth. He could visit Jason and Jenna in Vegas, sure, and they'd game together, an uncomfortable threesome, or maybe Jenna would invite a friend, maybe Corey would bring his own girl. Inside his head he was nuking an undead that wore Jenna's pretty face, and he felt bad about that, but better, too.

Like that time when he was a kid, following another kid around the apartment complex: everyone knew that the boy's parents had split and were moving out. He watched the kid shoot a respectable gob of spit from between pursed lips, watched it foam in the dirt, watched the kid poke at it with a red-striped straw picked up off the ground. Fascinated by the grossness of it, the used straw chewed and blackened, swarming with germs, dog piss or worse, Corey crouched close to look, and the kid thrust a fist against his cheek, twice and mean. The way the kid's mouth scrinched up tight as he backed away, still clutching the piece of plastic, the way he began to bawl convinced Corey not to go after him. It wasn't personal, Corey understood. The kid just needed someone to know how bad it felt to have no say in your own life.

Resting his elbows on his knees, Corey stared at A.J. laughing loudly in his expensive shirt and tie, A.J. who could make anything look effortless. When Jason had introduced them for the first time, back in middle school, Corey had fixated on the way A.J. held a cigarette so the glowing end was a living thing. He had studied the perfect rips in A.J.'s stovepipe-straight jeans that fit snugly in all the right places; it was messed up how he noticed these details, how in private he imitated A.J.'s pose.

Even years later, he was still following A.J.'s lead. He learned, by watching, how to pick up game-girls online: flatter them to pieces until a live one agreed to stop by the apartment, bust out the alcohol and let them choose his newest niche or AAA game, close the deal with a bonus round in the bedroom. Then send her on her way and do it again next week with someone else. So yeah, friend me, he had learned to be a boss player.

But life in the off-screen world was especially glitchy lately. Case in point: his Friday night date, Sinergie, demonstrated all the warmth of a stalactite in his king-sized bed, making it clear that her precious face and ass, top-notch features, he had to admit, were off-limits—as if he were unworthy. How awkwardly he had pumped away, balanced precariously on hands and toes, relaxing somewhat when she indicated it was okay to press his body against hers, even to maul her lopsided tits. How he had sweated to imagine her exotic, on-screen character, delicately muscled above an exaggeratedly indented waist, to feel something close to excitement. How she had remarked, afterward, lighting up without asking, that in person he was more orc than elf.

"You drooled on me," she coughed, exposing her prohibited tonsils, and when she was about to ash onto his new silk comforter, he had been a gentleman; he had removed the cigarette from her fingers and not bitch-slapped the untouchable, lacquered cheek and nose and eye. His brain had throbbed with how much he disliked her, but he managed to behave himself.

"Never pussy out, son," his father would say, sneaking up on him before school, landing a punch in his kidney. Over time, the pain slid into an absence of feeling that replaced even the hate. Words were just words, and he could step into the void, let the world's bullshit skate on by.

Now he smiled at Jason and his big chicken dreams, smiled wide like a rock star and said, "Cheers, mate," in the Aussie accent that earned him a chuckle, never mind he was losing everything that mattered, he was always good for a laugh, right? He sucked his sore front teeth, registered the pain, and let it slide.

———

Los Angeles, Paris, Amsterdam, Maui. Four cities in five months, each compounding her unhappiness. On the hotel's private inlet, Margaret felt her face settle into a scowl as she sat under an umbrella and watched her friends. Bride-to-be Jenna, seemingly unconcerned about The Day, body-surfed all the way up the scooped-out beach, laughed and jiggled handfuls of sand out of her gold lamé bikini bottoms. The boys crouched on rented boards and fell over themselves as they skated the ripples that scooted up the shore. If Margaret squinted her eyes, the three of them—Jenna in her gold swimsuit, plus Jason and Scott in their matching, banana-yellow board shorts—resembled sodden chunks of Cap'n Crunch cereal stuck to the inside of a white porcelain bowl. Now Margaret liked them better.

But Maui was a good place to catch her breath, to make plans. She felt as if she'd been running since December at USC, where her parents wouldn't stop complaining about the psychology degree she hadn't completed. Then to Paris, *beaucoup* bills thrown at the French immersion program she'd dropped out of, Madame's compositions when all she wanted to do was bum cigarettes from Théo at the Arc de Triomphe. Unable to speak to the young, frowning Frenchman, she'd made out with him instead, next to other couples hunched against the cold and swapping spit like brutes in a human zoo.

The memory of drawing in smoke from the damp, bitten end of his Gauloises, of fitting her lips into the warm declivity at the base of his throat, gave her shivers. Then Amsterdam, where her mother's friend had arranged the nanny job, and where there'd been that gorgeous rollercoaster ride with the husband. And now she was waiting in paradise for her best friend to get married already, waiting for Scott to say she could move in when she told him the news, hoping his beach house in San Clemente would be her last flop for a while.

She took off her sun hat and touched her hair, the cutest pixie cut her parents had paid for, in euros; she'd needed a real change, a transformation after everything that had happened. She crossed her eyes again at the waterlogged cereal-people, saw a thin piece with long, blonde hair give her the finger, and waved in return as the other nuggets somersaulted off their boards and into the sea. She felt content, a rare feeling, and wise at twenty-two to have the knowledge she had gained this morning.

She had gotten up early and driven to the drugstore for the pink litmus test, had peed on it and waited the correct amount of time, had felt the thrill of self-knowing rise and reach her heart when the reading was positive. It was one of the few positive things she could take credit for, and it filled her with warmth and purpose, gave her a reason for racing across the globe as if escaping from an assassin. She knew she could be great at this, great at being a mother, and as if in response, the barely-there baby flooded her body with light, partly *his*, had to be.

It shouldn't be too difficult convincing Scott that he was the father.

Perhaps she should tell him right away, back in their room and doing what he liked, wearing one of his t-shirts and a pair of his briefs. Not her favorite thing, she would feel humiliated and invisible, but she needed him to want her now, to feel affection for her. She craved this baby so badly her entire body hurt, and she'd even made deals with her childhood God. She despised hypocrites, but she'd been crying at night, sobbing for something to stop the contradiction of her heart, its acute ache: *Please let me have this and I will see only love.*

On the beach, she stretched out languorously, exposed her secret stomach and caught the lifeguard's stare. His sunglasses reflected nothing, his mouth remained set in its thick white line of zinc oxide, but she knew he took his mental photograph. She saw him as a reminder of what she was leaving behind, all the other SoCal guys, the temporary attachments, the need in her they couldn't reciprocate. Though at times it was delicious, like that Philosophy of Religion class she had walked out of, the way they wore the lifeguard's same expression as they watched her leave: eyes blank, mouths tight, wanting and hating her for being a rubber band girl no matter what they did to her, the way she snapped back into her own smooth, seductive shape.

The professor had been asserting that all human beings must choose—that every creature with a soul and an imagination must choose—to wrestle intelligently with the pain of knowledge and reject the bliss of ignorance. It made her restless, this talk of pain.

"I choose bliss," she whispered to the student at her side, sliding her crossed legs apart and exposing the tanned tops of her breasts as she leaned forward to gather her books. "Join me?"

He just stared, grim-lipped, and she took her time mounting the stairs to the top of the lecture hall, took her time pushing open the exit door, swallowed her desire to laugh. She wanted to take one more look, to see if the very hominoid professor had suffered any new knowledge by watching her short leather skirt ascend and recede, but she resisted.

Her unhappiness was almost behind her.

———

Corey was cold, in Maui. He opened the glass doors on the lanai of their suite; he and A.J. had gone whole hog in order to get lucky, the sunken tub with fourteen jets, the spectacular ocean view. Best men borrowing the maids of honor for an hour of dishonoring—wasn't that how it was done? Except since Sinergie, he'd been underwhelmed by the idea of it, so much work for a few seconds of feeling good and then wanting to ditch them as soon as possible, these girls who slept with whoever had the biggest wad of cash and stock options. Maybe he wanted what Jason had with Jenna, of course he did. It just seemed like all he was good for lately was using and getting used, the old Eurythmics song.

He turned on the heat, feeling foolish but aching with cold, his feet twin blocks of ice. A.J. had decided, at the last minute, not to bring work to the island. He was taking a surfing lesson, had urged Corey to take a break, too. Corey had agreed to lay off the trading but couldn't resist, in toto, the sweet company of his laptop. He watched as one enchanter mezzed a group of baddies into snoring swine. Minutes later, a tree-hag bazookaed mob after mob with her flaming roots. Good times.

But now that he was getting into the game, this new game, something puzzled him: in the blitzturf, a capture-the-flag wilderness in which the "flag" was a pneumatic, feisty female, in the fight between the heroic League and the repugnant, creeping Swarm, the Swarm always won. This made no sense to his algorithmic mind. When non-player characters were excluded, when a different group of real-life humans fought each other in every battle, how could it be? He decided to create a dark side character, a Swarmy blood-elf warlock with ass-kicking casting abilities, and find out for himself.

But when A.J. returned from the beach, sun-bronzed and more defined, somehow, a layer of office adipose having melted away in the Maui surf, Corey felt his brain sag in despair.

"I can't figure this infinity-loop winning streak, A.—the Swarm dudes are just, like, sincerely nice, polite guys with great gear. It's a programming fuckmare—" His fuse was lit, now. He was here for Jason, his best friend since elementary school, his wingman who had gotten Corey laid for the first time, but he'd been here eighteen hours and hadn't seen the guy once, hadn't glimpsed his chicken-eating grin for five fucking minutes. Like Corey didn't matter now that Jenna was in the picture, like he was back to being this skinny ginger-cream who got the shit beat out of him, like he wasn't six-four with a more or less six-figure salary who always had his friend's back, who paid for Jason's mangled Camaro even though Corey hadn't been there, who loved Jason like a brother, loved him.

Still holding his laptop, Corey stepped onto the lanai, looked out at the sea of nothingness. Now Jason was needing him gone, brah; he had his hot-wing hottie to keep him warm. Yo, leave your wedding gift—your bills, crystal egg timer, dick, whatever, in the Pukalani Room and don't let the double doors hit you in the back of your fat head, douchebag. Corey raised his computer, imagined slamming it against the concrete floor, turning it into silver and black confetti. He changed his mind and was about to put his fist through the glass door of the lanai when A.J. grabbed him from behind, locked his elbows, and muscled him into the Jacuzzi.

Cold water rained on his back, over his meaty arms with the half-sleeves of tats above the elbows, his reddish-blond curls, his eyebrows in thick slashes, the long, delicate nose he had inherited from his mother and somehow never broken.

"Dude, you need to get out of this room—make yourself pretty and meet me in the bar." Easing off, A.J. twisted the spigots closed and punched Corey in the back. Always, someone was beating on him. "Seriously, we're here for the best reason, right? Plus, it's island pussy gone wild out there, pineapple like you wouldn't believe. He who hesitates masturbates."

But it wasn't quite that plentiful, at least not when Corey walked into the Captain Hook Grotto. He'd shaved, put on a jacket, then realized he'd forgotten to pack any shoes besides flip-flops. These were Shrek-green, too, and gnarly with the blackened imprints of his toes. He'd changed his khakis for jeans, hoping to downplay the footwear, and kept his jacket on, praying for acceptable. But in the Grotto he felt underdressed. A couple of middle-aged women heavy with gold swayed over slim glasses topped with sprigs of mint; so much for the abundant p. But there was A.J., and Jason. His pulse sped up, he was so grateful to see his friend. There was also this other guy, blonde-stubbled, greenish-gold eyes, so obviously Jenna's twin that Corey could smell the deep fryer wafting out of his pores.

Jason pulled a chair for Corey and patted his face with affection. Corey couldn't help breaking into his happy-dog grin, practically wagging his tail with the deeply good feeling.

"How ya doing, man?" Jason smiled back. "Meet Scott, Jenna's dizygotic brother."

The kid, Scott, tall and well-built, stood and shot a perfect white smile in Corey's direction. His fingers reached for Corey's hand and abruptly, Corey's good feeling was gone. The kid's eyes were unfocused. They'd been throwing back shots of tequila, and in front of Scott were stacked six empties.

"Scott just got great news," Jason deadpanned. "He's gonna be a dad."

Corey watched Jason and A.J. exchange a look, burst out laughing. A.J. slapped Scott on the back as if the kid had just scored a winning touchdown, then he ordered another round. Trying to catch up, Corey asked for a beer and a shot, saw Scott's eyes roll with distaste.

"I hate babies and I hate beers," Scott slurred. "Smell makes me so, so…" His yellow head flopped down toward Corey's feet then bobbed back up, a weird grin cracking his face open. "Those some sick kicks, man…"

Corey downed half his beer and stared at Scott's throat, all stringy, glottal cords. He saw his hand reaching around that neck, squeezing it quiet and making those deadly, drunk eyes, same as Jenna's, pop and go blank.

"Here's the good part," A.J. swallowed his alcohol and winced. "Good part's she's a Victoria's Secret type, I shit you not. Moms gone wild, right, Scottie?"

Scott's handsome face looked swollen, bee-stung.

A.J. continued, "But the *best* part, best part's she's loaded—parents in petroleum, right? So all Scottie's gotta do is the prenup shuffle, play it cool—not that there's anything wrong with living off the Colonel's secret recipe and the bird that will not fly, but we're talking POTUS-league here, par-tay in the West Wing and all that comes—"

Scott threw a hand over A.J.'s mouth, cleared his throat to speak. Corey thought the kid looked unwell in the grainy light leaking from the green and gold beer signs, the yellows of Scott's eyes reflecting the plastic pirate torches, his cheeks and lips scalded-looking, red as raw meat.

"Problem is—" Scott coughed, flexing his tongue as if his teeth were in the way, "she's a ho."

Corey watched the kid's fingers slide off A.J.'s face and realized, the knowledge hitting him squarely in the chest and moving down his body as the beer and tequila got into his blood, that Scott was a boy-lover, a homo-fucking sapien. Did the guys know? Did the girlfriend know? Corey felt gypped, the butt of their joke, out of the loop. He watched with agitation as Scott's fingers plucked at A.J.'s collar, smoothing out invisible creases, but he couldn't look away. He felt a belch rise and fill his esophagus with the beer smell that Scott detested, and despite his growing disgust for the kid, he breathed it out of his nostrils, kept his mouth shut.

"So here's the rub, dude." Jason looked straight at Corey, a request in his eyes—don't pussy out over this—"Scott's gonna be my best man. No hard feelings, right, brah? Take one for the team, and I'll catch you next time." Jason winked, and Corey was confused. Next time? But the information sank in—he looked at Scott, a thief like Jenna, both of them snatching at his happiness—two snatches, foul and deceitful.

He ordered another beer, another shot, and emptied both. Then Scott's face was next to his, too close, his mouth screwed up and saying, "Corree, my bro, you unnerstand, you gonna take it like a man, right?"

Those yellow, devilish eyes—blood-elf eyes, warlock eyes—

narrowed as if in a swoon, and suddenly Scott's obscenely red lips pressed clumsily against his, but this couldn't be happening, it was like getting beat on, someone always beating on him. Corey's dad holding a three-hundred-pound barbell over his head, threatening to let go: "You can do another one, Cor, don't pussy out on me," the aggressive veins in his father's neck, Corey forcing himself to grip the metal bar, to heave the weight up and ignore the muscle in his bicep ripping, shearing like a piece of meat, he was not just a piece of meat. The feel of Scott's tongue, cool and erotic. The taste of tequila, sour and bitter. Corey used his shoulder to butt their bodies apart, hard, seized Scott by the neck and squashed his face sideways against the bar.

"You'll forgive me, right, Corree? We'll see you at the altar, right?" Scott smiled crookedly at the ceiling and flung his hand in Corey's direction, knocked over a bowl of pretzels shaped in an unfamiliar alphabet. The hand stayed extended, stiff and earnest, as A.J. extracted Scott, all slippery, floppy limbs, and began to steer him toward the exit. The room was a ship, swaying, and hadn't Jason seen what just… Moments were sliding into each other too rapidly. There were gaps in the floor, in the walls, in the evening, and Corey strained to see straight.

He heard Jason's voice, almost gone, calling out, "Get some shut eye," then A.J. adding, "Till we do it again," and when Corey could see where he was, alone, his heart thudded as his cold, blunted fingers clenched into fists. His head burned, and he felt around his stung, numb mouth with a tongue gone thick and dumb, tasting blood, tequila, something ugly and familiar that caught at the back of his throat.

———

Margaret sank into a chaise in the hotel lobby and closed her eyes. Was it only twelve hours since she had told Scott almost everything, since he had stared at her in shock, then suspicion, then told her they were over, done, before going out drinking with his new besties? He'd come back late and passed out, and she'd slept reasonably well despite his getting up twice to puke his guts out. He'd made it to the bathroom both times, and she'd wiped his face with a warm towel, but he hadn't changed his mind.

This morning, at last the morning of the wedding, she felt as if she were running a low fever. She needed to lie here for a few minutes and replay the highlights of the past months, searching for the scenes, like the best parts of a favorite film, that would soothe her and tell her what she needed to do next. Instead, she saw her mother's high cheekbones, the dark bangs ironed into finger waves that backed off her forehead as if in alarm.

Mother had stayed connected to her Dutch friend, a gregarious woman she had met in Borneo before Margaret was born. For two years, their husbands had measured the impact of drilling on sea turtles, of emissions on butterflies; Margaret had been surprised to learn that big oil hired men to do these things. After Margaret's failure in Paris, Mother contacted this friend, whose married son lived in Amsterdam.

"Hedge funds!" her mother announced, voice brimming with approval of the son's genius choice, adding that the young family desperately needed a nanny for their unruly twins. "Like Scott and Jenna," Mother described over the phone. "Spoiled, a bit, but younger, of course! But so adorable, already such strong little personalities, it's easy to see why Greetje and Bas let them run wild. Cookies and treats whenever they want, that sort of thing. Greetje—Dutch for Margaret—your soul sister!—manages a travel agency, and Bas works at home but needs his breaks. Room and board, just until you re-enroll, and spending money, of course. Just until school starts next fall. Be happy, darling, and don't get fat. The Dutch like to put candy and sausage in everything!"

Margaret had wanted to stay longer in Paris with her friends, busking in the Metro, because they were so nice to her, feeding her chocolate croissants for breakfast and calling her their *chouchou*. But she saw the end of it before they were halfway through, how sleeping on the floor of their flat would soon lose its charm. She made the single phone call when the cold began to last all day, penetrating even through her cashmere coat.

She had wanted, for once, to do what her mother asked and get it right; even so, the contrast from French bohemia to Dutch conservatism was a shock. Bas and Greetje lived on the edge of Amsterdam in a condominium that imitated its seventeenth century, downtown brothers and sisters only in that rooms were stacked upon rooms. Everything in this part of the city was new in neat, measured lines, like living in an Ikea store. Her room and bath were on the fourth floor, and the hot water often ran out before it reached her.

But as promised, she fell in love with the four-year-old twins, Esmé and Henrik, who gave her gifts when she arrived: Esmé, gummy licorice warmed in her fist, and Henrik, a bright yellow shoelace. Taking them to the canals after eating lunch in the train station became her favorite routine. As the commuters moved through in surges, in silver-gray suits and scarves, in striking, unsmiling faces, Margaret was a calm boat, a safe mooring for her miniature sailors. In the station, the Dutch looked so industrious, carrying their space within them instead of spreading it around messily. The Dutch kept their houses shipshape and their ground-floor curtains open, flowers and porcelain on display. But their personal business remained private, reserved for higher, interior rooms.

She had liked walking with a child on each side of her, pulling them in tightly like ducklings as bicycles sped past over cobblestones, over ice, even in the rain. After a morning of sampling cheese and *stroopwafels* in the outdoor market, she liked taking the train back to the end of the line, Henrik fidgety but tiring, ready for his nap, Esmé banging her head against Margaret's shoulder, letting Margaret braid and unbraid her soft, tangled hair. Except for their occasional, childish violence—Esmé head-butting her in enthusiasm over a plastic hippo, bruising Margaret's nose and drawing tears of pain—the children were to die for.

Greetje was also lovely, clear-eyed, kind and organized, always dressed in skirts that showed off her slim legs and fertile hips. Her husband, Bas, was good-looking in a way that cameras couldn't capture, in a way Margaret felt rather than saw. So began the problem: in how Bas felt. Or probably Margaret was the problem. Her mother's comment rang true, spoken after she had pierced her eyebrow, after she had tattooed the side of her neck, "Always Margaret who takes things too far."

It had started during lunch. Bas came downstairs to spend time with the little ones over soup, bread with butter, chamomile tea. Sitting across the table from him, Margaret had tried to bring the soup spoon to her mouth, but each time, the utensil shook forcefully in her hand. Without a word, Bas got up and sat beside her, near enough to close the circuit between them. He pulled Henrik onto his lap and made a game out of the meal while Esmé, a mini Greetje, adored her daddy-who-made-everything-fun. In this way, with Bas next to her, Margaret could eat, could breathe.

Then later, when the children were tucked in for their naps, she tried not to think as she climbed the stairs to Bas's room, stood before his door and forced her hand to turn the knob, forced her body to walk in. She stood there trembling, not daring to look at his face but feeling him looking at her, radiating more than looking. Her hands were at her sides, the palms turned outward to him in supplication. Her mouth quavered—prettily, she hoped—as if she were about to cry.

Without hesitation, Bas got up and walked past her, barely brushed her fingers with his own, and shut the door. The next few moments were a fluxing, chemical rush as he kissed her mouth to calm her, undressed them both and was inside her, his warm skin making up for all the frigid showers.

Afterward, she had thought, how like the Dutch to know what she needed and then give it to her so efficiently, generously, sweetly. Dutch engineers had created land out of sea, had mastered the wind, had designed a government that encouraged children to be born and more importantly, to thrive, and she experienced the freedom of Dutch ingenuity when Bas was loving her, everywhere, like bicycle tires spinning, joyous industry.

After two blissful months she had returned to the states as her mother had decreed. More than her own family she had loved them, all of them: sweet Greetje, Esmé, Henrik. But leaving Bas, the Bas she had come to think of as hers, left a hole in her brain that made no sense.

She remembered Bas the last time she had seen him, standing in the doorway of his tall house, diaper bag in hand. He was the embodiment of male domesticity and of everything *gezellig*—homey, inviting—that she had luxuriated in, taken as her due. She didn't want to consider that what happened between them had happened before, would happen again with the next nanny; she must believe he would go on setting the molecules around him into warming light. He would "do investing," and Greetje would send people on extraordinary journeys, and Esmé and Henrik would grow up to be as bright and resilient as their parents. That Margaret had something of his—the new life in her body had to be his—was like possessing, finally, the secret knowledge that everyone wanted.

This brightness and resilience were what she could wish for Jenna, and for herself, when she stood at her best friend's side to witness her marriage vows.

———

Shoes motherfucking shoes. Corey was at his laptop, just a few hours before the wedding, just enough time to play a couple rounds in the blitzturf before the show, then gotta get some shoes. It almost didn't matter since he wasn't going on stage, on the proscenium he thought it was called or maybe he was thinking of ancient theaters, not chapels; anyway, the point was, he wouldn't be going up there at all. He wouldn't be up there, so nobody would be looking at his feet, so what did it matter except he wouldn't disrespect Jason, had promised not to pussy out.

But now what—his password wasn't working. He had no choice but to wait, impatiently, for the next available technician, or dig into the code himself, and there wasn't time either way. He decided to dig anyhow.

Then he was wandering the hotel lobby in confusion, looking for the boutique store he remembered seeing when he checked in. Silk ties and hand-painted scarves, lurid high heels and loafers, he thought, cracking his knuckles repeatedly. Upstairs, the computer gaped like a mouth hanging open, screen smashed to bits. He'd broken a drinking glass in the process, cut his hand and arm, but he was free of the beast, that Sisyphean rock that was one less tie to his so-called friends who had treated him like a child, had humored him when he'd called to tell them he'd been hacked. By a sincerely nice, polite, Swarmy technocrat, through keylogger most likely, damn hackhead asshole stealing his keystrokes, his heavy metal elf left standing in nothing but panties, the guild bank gutted.

Here he was again with that too-familiar feeling, that it was all a big sack of nothing, all the hours, months, *years* they had spent together, the three of them. Nobody had *his* back, everyone had let him down—he had a line-up in his head, a backlog of bullshit he wished he could put in his sights and obliterate: A.J. on a surfboard, lips curved in a grin that was an insult, abs glistening with sea water; Jason with his worthless promises, *catch you next time*; Scott's handsome face looming, eyes open, moving in for the kill; his old man's gritty cheek pressing close as the weight dropped, over and over, *take it like a man, son.* When he thought he could at least get good at getting the girl, whatever girl, and he'd come up empty there, too.

He maneuvered around a waterfall and saw her, Scott's girlfriend, recognized her right away. Sleek yet top heavy in a close-fitting dress, the material silky-looking so that he wanted to rub it between his fingers. Her eyes closed in a daydream, Scott's mouth—he forced the image away with the same rage he had let loose moments ago, murdering his computer.

A plan took shape, what he needed. Still high on adrenaline, giddy as a little girl! he laughed at himself, straightened his shoulders, walked over to the girlfriend, showed some teeth, his mother always said he had a beautiful smile so use it, don't scare her.

"Miss? I'm here for the wedding, Jason's—a friend of the groom, and I sure could use a woman's eye." He sounded like trash, begging, *sure could use? A woman's eye?* But she sat up and smiled, held herself like a fairy princess, like that Jenna. Corey didn't think she was all that, not the way A.J. made her out to be, but she was fuckable, he could make himself do it.

"Pleased to make your acquaintance," she purred, indulging him, and he got it, she liked to play along.

They picked out a pair of preppy oxfords in honey-brown, and he invited her to his "sweet" suite, for champagne. She accepted with an actual peal of laughter. It was on.

Upstairs, he tried to be civil, not sure what he was doing. Still the helpless but charming oaf, he overfilled a glass then spilled it down his shirtfront. Shirtless and peripherally aware of how this must look, he downed half the bottle without meaning to; the sight of his abused laptop made him feel wondering and stupid, furious. She hadn't even lifted her glass, and he didn't know why she was in his room.

Moving toward Margaret, he looked down at his hands as he placed them on her dress. His large, sore fingers, so recently striated with his own blood, dwarfed the hook-and-eye closure, the tiny metal tongue of the zipper that parted the fabric, like a second skin, from her body. He buried his face in the dress and pushed down with both arms until she was on the floor beneath him. She just lay there, their two bodies magnetized to repel each other, a replay of goddamn Sinergie so that a hurt sound came out of his mouth—how he hated them all.

He took off his belt and she began to fight him, finally; he clamped his hand over her mouth and struggled out of his pants, into her waxen and unyielding body. He shut his eyes and worked at it, finding a rhythm, but it wasn't what he wanted, so he flipped her over like a coin. He forced his fingers into her mouth, levered his elbow under her knee and pulled up hard, laid flesh into flesh—now she was waking up, now she was starting to feel, pinned and gagged, like a pulsing animal.

Her body twisted as he pressed his face between her shoulder blades, breathed the acrid scent of her armpits, almost a boy's smell, stroked the masculine tattoo on the side of her neck, grabbed the back of her head where the hair was cut short, coarse and bristling. He heard himself snarl, his visceral, primitive brain uncoiling with pleasure, perceiving her as a boy-creature with her musky, scared odor, her weak and flopping boy arms and boy legs. This feeling grew, unwelcome but irresistible, spawning images of a long, lean-hipped body caught under his until he could believe it, could picture Scott beneath him, Scott making injured animal sounds, Scott shivering helplessly, and Corey wasn't cold now, his muscles were warm and oiled and he could do this, finish this thing and feel good about it.

He took his time, then, he even cried out, a sound shot through with agony, and in the midst of it, as he ground Scott to pieces, he became almost considerate; his hand stroked the boy's cheek and closed eyelid that flattened against the hotel carpet.

Afterward, he recognized the female again, how easy it was to see her, and he felt shame too rapidly obscuring the last pangs of pleasure. He could appreciate the doll-nature of her body now that it had resumed its shape, and he smoothed her head and crumpled dress.

Afterward, always there were consequences. But the doll who was also a ho, her own boyfriend had said so, was soon gone, walked out on her own two feet, a little dazed, maybe, but not whining or blubbering. And hadn't A.J. said something last night about her liking it that way, weren't they talking about, right before Scott—he felt a sob rise in his throat, an acid surge in his stomach, remorse choking him, also something like longing.

He cleaned up, felt better, maybe. Put on his good shirt, his used-to-be-best-man's suit. Felt the rage still there, just around the curve. Heard the door lock behind him, every sound magnified, as he walked toward the elevator, steered his brain forward. It was the wedding hour, kids, D-Day. Time to play nice.

The shoes looked good, he wouldn't embarrass himself.

———

Margaret had assumed Corey was one of the good guys, that she and he were on the same team. This was the friend Jenna and Jason liked to talk about, the one they made excuses for; Corey was the gentle giant, the shy, insecure guy with a heart of gold. Margaret had heard them say, too, that Corey could be a big baby, Corey was a ladies' man as long as A.J. was there to put it in, that sort of thing, but always their last words were about trust: Corey was the guy you wanted on your side when you'd had one too many and said the wrong thing to the wrong asshole. Now that Scott had turned against her, maybe Corey was the one who could put things right.

She had trusted him, was even impressed by his suite, and had begun to wake up only when he started chugging the champagne she turned down. But as her mother had warned, the moment you walk through their door, it's done—that's that. So she had watched, fascinated, as his lips fastened on the bottle and the liquid poured down his throat; he *was* a giant, an ogre king in his metallic-threaded jacket and reddish-blond stubble, the bottle tiny in his hands that had grown as she stared, that had turned into grasping, prying weapons. And yet she had been unprepared for his advances, unprepared for how familiar they felt, for hadn't she been here before? Wasn't this the kind of thing she did, had done with even Jason the night before she fled to Europe, displayed her charms before her friends' boyfriends, husbands, best men?

Corey wasn't going to be the best man anymore, of course she had already known. This made it better, at first, when she couldn't breathe and couldn't feel, like she was making up for something. She could hear him growling, almost, as he drove on and on, his body furious, the intensity and weight of him pounding an idea into her, something she must be careful of, something she must keep safe. If this was what he needed, if this would balance the scales, she could bear him.

Except he wanted her to feel him. When the pain finally got through, knocking the breath back into her, paralyzing terror came with it. Light crashed into the room and blinded her, her body grated against the carpet as against steel wool, his hand on her neck was a vise, his smell was blood. She focused all her attention on what was inside her, this baby they were making…had made…that *she* had made…with Bas…with Bas…

She had made it, was there, staring blankly at Jenna and Jason, at the mountains of floral decorations, at the minister with a silver watch chain glinting beneath his robes. Standing across from Scott—"You're next!" Jenna mouthed, winking—watching the promises pour like smoke from between Jenna's lips, then Jason's, in a repetitive stream. Jason looking serious and sincere. Jenna extra-floaty after swallowing a Xanax, not that anyone would notice. Margaret hadn't taken hers—birth defects—hadn't explained the blush-colored stripes across her neck and chest that might have passed for sloppily applied sunscreen.

She steadied herself by focusing on Scott's cufflinks, pale blue aquamarines. She willed the blue into her head, soft baby blue on the walls of a little boy's room, the Hawaiian sky over Jenna and Jason, two as one.

If she pushed her eyes in the direction of the front row, she could see the outline of Corey's body in its tall and big suit, the light reflected off his shoes. These were proof of their awful connectedness, and they repulsed her as much as if he had somehow forced his feet into overlarge, brown palmetto bugs. She didn't want to see him, and her eyes complied. Through her tears, his face remained a blur.

She staggered into the reception with a brain-nausea rolling through her, her vision still impaired. She felt an almost supernatural awareness of Corey's proximity, and although other faces came into view, he remained two blackened pits attached to something that hulked over the crowd.

When A.J. pulled her onto the dance floor, she felt the blur lurch toward her but pass through them. Her legs shook as if she had just run a marathon, she was hot under her armpits and between her thighs. Soon the father of the bride cut in, and Margaret felt herself relax for a moment; it was such a relief to be held. She wanted to tell him everything. She had known this man since she and Jenna were little, and he knew her like his own daughter, knew she, too, had a right to happiness.

As they circled the dance floor, he said the thing he always said, "You're the heroine of my favorite poem, you know, the one about Goldengrove unleaving, lovely Margaret."

His words meant everything and nothing to her. He spoke about the joy of gaining a son, and soon, as well, a daughter? She thought he would have recognized the distance between her and Scott, the new, obvious distance, but he didn't. Then he danced with Jenna, their heads bent together, Jenna in her quilled bodice and matching headpiece, the colonel and his fabulously feathered daughter. Occasionally, they glanced at her.

The song changed. Jenna began her approach with rapid steps and flailing wings, taking forever to push through the crowd. Margaret could see how her friend's elongated nails, like claws, were twisting nervously, her plumed brow rutted with alarm. Now she knows, Margaret thought. Everything and nothing.

The lights were brighter now, she was back in the hotel room, back with Jason, with Bas, with Scott, with Corey, always with Corey, now. She was changing, becoming the same as Corey, a blurred-out place for pain, anger, and shame to hole up, so deep and distorted that everything else was blotted out. Margaret forced her arms to thrust Jenna back, her mouth to say, *I'm sorry, I'm so sorry.*

As she spoke, her mouth and eyes kept melting the way everything was melting, spinning, changing. The music became louder, a synthesized female voice repeating against a transparent, shimmering membrane of sound, words that made no sense. Light jumped out of the dance hall like something alien and ground itself against her eyes; she was with Corey, inside Corey as the light grabbed Jenna and took her away.

She was with Corey, on the floor in a room in a building on a street in a city on an island in a country on a planet in a galaxy endless with stardust. Out there, knowing didn't matter. Where the darkness was traveling, where the darkness was not pain, not sex, not love, where the darkness was her baby, she could have stayed forever.

Her knees hit the carpet. She felt the awful clench and contraction of the universe. Out of the spinning, a planet came into focus, then a continent and a country, an island and a city, a street and a building. Inside the building was a room in which she knelt, understanding what she had chosen.

SALT

THAT FALL, before I even met him, several body parts were affected: my inner ear attacked by vertigo, caused by vigorous, late-summer swimming; my forehead, exfoliated daily, broken out in bumps under new, brisk bangs; my elbow over-loofahed into a raw, swollen lump that required antibiotics. Enthusiastically, I was trying to fix something, a sloppiness that was one part inattention and three parts desire. When I looked up the word "enthusiasm," I took its meaning to be "lost in one's God," which explained my zeal for Jeremiah. It is obvious, looking back, that my hands led me to him, and my knee brought us—me, at least—to something like truth.

In September I started two jobs, making ice cream and managing a box office, which helped pay for the final three courses I needed to graduate. The year before, my degree had been tweaked to allow one semester in San Sebastián, Spain, and, as it turned out, in Biarritz, France, most weekends, where the beachgoers were closer to my age and the baguettes tasted better. Neither city had a drinking age, and both had nightclubs, so my friends and I spent more time imbibing and dancing than on our studies. I emerged with a taste for cigarettes, an aversion to vodka, unable to speak either country's language to any appreciable degree, and a semester short of acceptable credits.

When I tied on a blue apron at White Glacier, I concentrated solely on ice cream. I brewed pots of coffee and added quarts of cream, ladles of vanilla, cups of sparkling sugar. I alternated the ice and rock salt layers as instructed, two and a half feet high inside the stainless-steel cylinder. Each time the cylinder slowed its spinning, I reached into the freezing, salty slush, down to the very bottom, and used my fingertip to push that one diamond of salt out of the slot-and-groove mechanism. I smiled from my window in the glass observation booth and handed out freshly made samples to passersby. The season's basketball stars stopped by regularly, helping to mitigate the job's geek factor. How collegiate it was, or appeared to be, to support your education by hoop or by scoop; how adorable when a young girl served up a taste of a jock's sweet future in a tiny pink spoon.

Then, at the fifty-seven-seat Armenian Playhouse, I became the consummate ticket seller. Animated and informative, I lied that the current performance was a real winner since it featured Equity actors (retired), a playwright verging on fame (bankruptcy), and a director acclaimed in several countries (all in conflict with U.S. interests). For a long time, I hoped that fifty-seven held some cultural significance, but it turned out to be simply the number of folding chairs that fit in the building pursuant to the fire code. On weeknights when the fire marshal was unlikely to visit, I unfolded the illicit fifty-eighth chair and stayed to watch the first scene of the second act. I sometimes accompanied the wardrobe mistress in her platform clogs and sequined, velvet skirt to her favorite jazz bar where I learned to appreciate the restorative effect of an ice-cold gin martini.

I tried to like jazz but didn't get it. My ear bones would rebel and whisper messages to my other bones to clank and sigh and ache in a way that demanded ibuprofen instead of communion. Music that inspired a different kind of longing was my kryptonite, songs by Robert Plant and Elton John, David Bowie and Dave Gahan, a gushy medley of boy need that I listened to on headphones while reconciling the

Armenian cash box or, early the next morning, gallons of Glacial syrups and purees.

One morning at the Glacier, I was mixing up a drum of Rich Dutch Chocolate and noticed that the laces on my nearly new, leather K-Swiss tennis shoes were disintegrating. I changed them out, but a week later I watched another pair pull apart. This time I was standing over the drain in the center of the tiled floor of the ice-cream room, the rounded toe of my sneaker slopped over, as usual, with melted ice and salt that fell in sheets from the just-churned canisters. After another week, my hands began to itch like crazy, and a red discoloration encircled the base of each finger. My right hand, the one I regularly plunged into freezing brine to fit nubbin-into-slot, was more seriously aggravated. A doctor called it dermatitis and gave me the requisite prescription for cortisone cream. When I asked him what else I should do, he told me to quit my job. I found that holding my hands under hottest tap water provided temporary relief, and I was reassigned to the waffle cone iron with its companion can of Pam cooking spray. I soon developed a sebaceously glistening t-zone that could at least have reflected customers' smiles so I wouldn't have to. I retained my assistant manager title, but if I couldn't make ice cream, what was the point?

I compensated by eating more of it. Each night I'd take home the eight ounces we were allowed, plus a few spoons extra, and cram the carton full of mix-ins. Sometimes I'd smuggle out a quart to get though a day off. Pumpkin, an autumn-only flavor, was my favorite, and packed with peanut butter cups, it became my salvation and shame. Arriving home after midnight to my rented room, I'd eat the entire quart in slow, languorous bites, taking breaks only to scald my maddening hands. I was hungry for pleasure; I'd tried to throw up once or twice, but the ice cream always refused to leave my body. If I felt a little sluggish on the days following these binges, I'd temporarily switch to Vanilla Custard Lite with smashed Heath Bars. My hair, though, seemed fuller and shinier, and when I piled it high on my head like a crown, customers were more likely to tip.

I had seen Jeremiah a couple of times when he stopped by the Glacier, looking for Sarah, and I couldn't get him out of my head. Today I was sitting near the poncho man, a campus fixture who played only Beatles on a piano with wheels, staring at my hands. The red parts were starting to turn white and flake off, and the skin underneath was shiny and tight—what healing looked like, I supposed, or second-degree burns. I was dressed inappropriately for class in shorts and a threadbare t-shirt, trying to absorb the October sun. I noticed a shadow fall over my lace-less sneakers, and when I looked up, there was Jeremiah. Seeing him anywhere but at the Glacier felt surreal, and it took me a moment to recognize him.

"Hiya!" He was all merriment and good looks, his rough edges disappearing in the sunlight. "Is this what you do for fun?"

Jeremiah was part actor, which disarmed me; I saw him playing the hippie dude with facial hair like frosting that I wanted to scrape off—I didn't want to hurt him, just lick him. He was another pretty boy hanging out, scooting along the back streets on a longboard while his girlfriend, Sarah, sweated twelve-hour shifts, six days a week, as co-manager of the Glacier.

Anyone could see what he saw in her, Sarah Braithwaite, matching blonde, sturdy of limb and stout of heart, book-smart and street-smart, forgiving, organized, at peace with her situation in the city across from the City. Sarah's lineage went back to the Mayflower, to descendants who launched their community in Maine, built some of the first composting toilets, and lived off the land before migrating west, settling on Oregon. These had been matter-of-fact, Earth-friendly people before it was fashionable to be so, and while Sarah hadn't been so lucky as to avoid personal misfortune—both her parents died when she was fifteen, and she raised her younger brother and sister single-handedly (Jeremiah claimed she could do literally anything with one hand tied behind her back)—she had inherited a savings fund, a strong immune system, and a can-do attitude that fit as comfortably as her perfectly worn (but too short and too tight across the rear) blue jeans. I couldn't help but admire her.

Sarah was obviously busy, at the store day and night. Jeremiah, however, seemed to have unlimited free time.

I told him I liked to bike across the Bridge and go hiking—I mentally searched my closet for the Salvation Army hiking boots I'd worn only once. His eyes flicked up and down my bare legs encouragingly, and I continued to speak like an automaton, like I was delivering a rehearsed dialogue about White Glacier's newest flavor: "Alotta Colada's sweet cream base bursts with coconut and macadamia chunks in a ribbon of tangy-smooth pineapple puree." I bragged about my swimming, how I swam laps all summer at the gym. I left out the part about the vertigo.

"And I go mountain biking with friends from work, which is really great. Until we took this downhill pass where I went over my handlebars and broke my fall with my hands." He quickly took these in his own and examined them with real tenderness.

His touch unnerved me. I couldn't help but think of Sarah, then, how "Tangysmooth" became the Glacier's nickname for co-manager number one while Sarah was dubbed, more plainly and dearly, "Sweetcream."

I forced myself to go on: "I mean, that was like a month ago. There was blood, but everyone was really nice about it, revealing their own biking scars as badges of honor. This is something else—not contagious, though."

"Poor hands," he said. "Let's go biking, hiking, and swimming— that'll help them. You'll be my triathlon girl. Are you free on Friday?"

And so our sporting dates began. We'd meet outside the locker rooms, change, ride our bikes out of town and struggle up the hillsides. Sometimes we'd hike down to the beach, and sometimes we'd just climb to a rock and sit. Back on campus, we'd jump in the pool, shower, meet again outside the locker rooms, grab a bite and then part ways. These were long days of many hours spent together, just the two of us, alone, witnessed only in the lap lanes of the campus pool, perhaps, by flippered students who surfaced for a second to hit the back wall with a twisting kick. When we ate burgers together, people might have noticed how I stared at his impressive mess of hair, trying not to linger over my fries but having nowhere else I needed to be.

At work, I guiltily avoided saying anything to Sarah. What would I say? "Hey, I'm seeing your boyfriend once a week; we sweat and eat together. He talks about his other friends, who all seem to be female, but he never mentions you." In fact, he did talk about her, giving her the authority of a hippie wife, mentioning her so casually it seemed they were unquestionably entwined—they had met in Eugene and moved together from that college town to ours; she was his Mama, and he was her Papa. With his next breath, he'd mention a concert he was going to with Kate, or last night's party with Lexy, or the band McKayla sang in. Who were these women? Would he ever ask me out on a Saturday night, or were Fridays before five my only allotted timeslot? Were our "triathlons" equal to, or lesser than, a midnight showing of *The Rocky Horror Picture Show*? A late picnic dinner at the beach? Clubbing in the City, followed by a motorcycle ride to the bluffs to watch the sunrise? If he invited me to go jockstrap shopping, as long as it was during the evening, I thought I would accept in an instant.

Once, at the Armenian Playhouse, I ran into a former scooper who claimed to have known Jeremiah well. She—of course she was a she—said he was a private school dropout, the only boy among seven sisters, a talented musician, a street-corner heckler, a closet misogynist. She said he was a "terrifying flirt" or a "terrible introvert," her words garbling as she kept naming his contradictions. He was "an impulsive giver with empty pockets," "loyal and flaky, both," and "badly groomed with a great nose for scents." How did she know him? She said they had met in church, but she never understood why he liked to wear his short, dark hair in those four crazy ponytails. At this, I stopped listening. Clearly, hers was a different Jeremiah.

One day after a hike followed by burgers, he offered me a ride home on his motorcycle. "Oh, no thank you," I said. I'd have to leave my bicycle on campus and catch a bus back in the morning. But he insisted, and I relented, and although nothing happened when he arrived in front of the little house that held my little room, I thought of him all afternoon, all night. I had simply given him a brief hug, thanked him again, and halfway fell off his jump seat because my thighs had gone numb. But for days thereafter, I imagined what would happen the next time, how he'd ask to come in and there we'd be, alone with only a chair and the floor and a bed. How we'd melt like soft serve, his agile, bike-and-swim-sturdy limbs devoted entirely to my paths and lanes. In my daydreams, I planned our recreation single-mindedly with enthusiastic, romantic passivity.

An early rain came in November, and on streets slick with water and motor oil, at dusk, I braked halfway through a long downhill turn and crashed my bike. I was about to be late for the Armenian theater and took the turn too fast; I hit the pavement with the left side of my body and skidded a couple of feet into traffic, shredding my jeans. Still I rode on, arriving wet and shaken but on time, then sold tickets until I noticed my knee was swollen to twice its normal size. Riding home in the dark on the still-wet streets, I wobbled uphill along the road where I had fallen, afraid that if I stopped, my tires would slip and the accident would repeat itself. In the morning, I went to the campus clinic and received infrared therapy treatments and a list of rehabilitative exercises that included using a stationary bicycle.

When Friday arrived, I limped to our meeting place outside the locker rooms. As soon as Jeremiah saw my knee, he knelt, reaching around to hold my leg with both hands, and kissed it. I thought I'd die with how sexy he looked, loving my broken knee, the flesh battered in my stupid, careless haste. I had again hurt my body by not paying careful attention to it, and here he was, showing me how to be gentle, how to take it easy.

"Poor knee," he said, his hands still touching me, and these were the warmest, most inviting words I had ever heard.

We met again when I had mostly healed, but I was stiff and awkward on the bike, fearful of re-injuring myself, and we didn't ride very far. Swimming afterward was playful and therapeutic, and we chased each other under water in obvious amphibious foreplay. We came out of our locker room doors at the same time and sat together to put on our shoes. Our hair was wet, making it look as if we had showered together. He leaned his back against mine, using me for resistance to help pull on clean socks, and then he put his arm around my shoulders, casually, but long enough for me to relax against him, to pretend. We both moved slowly—perhaps, like me, he didn't want to rush the moment. At last it seemed the thing between us had begun for real, had deepened. In my poor heart, I was certain he would have me.

We went to FatBurger as a matter of course, as any couple might go to their favorite hangout.

"I'll take you home," he said, his mouth full.

"You don't have to," I said, playing with the salt and pepper shakers. "It's okay, I've got my bike."

"Just let me take you."

"No, really, I'm out of your way…"

Still chewing, he flopped his head across folded arms, gold curls everywhere. Exhausted. His women were wearing him out.

"Just. Let. Me." He mumbled it through the food in his mouth, through all of that hair. And I found him irresistible. I wanted to place my head beside his on the table, to tell him something smart and fun, to be light and silly so he would keep spending time with me. But nothing came out of my mouth; my hands wouldn't touch him the way I wanted them to.

When he looked up at me, finally, wearily, with a question in his eyes—when I should have said, simply, "Yes," I didn't. I said nothing.

"You are so damn guilty all the time!" he hissed, rising, and his words scared me, because I knew he was right. This guilt was anger twisted inside-out, anger at the part of me that kept faking neutrality, that was so scared of rejection I couldn't act on what I wanted. I had tried to appear laidback and self-aware, witty enough to describe my silly disappointments in a way that made them sound interesting—that made *me* sound interesting—but it was all a lie. I would willingly lie down for him—anywhere, anytime—but I would never be able to tell him so.

In a second, I found a scapegoat: Sarah. I was guilty because Sarah let her man run around; Sarah didn't care if he made women fall in love with him. Sarah let him do whatever he wanted, and in return, he kept coming back to her. Hating Sarah almost obliterated my guilt.

"Take me home, then," I said. I tried to sound seductive and sure of myself. I hoped he would ignore my flush of embarrassment and hear my passion, my directness, my guarantee. But he was finished with me, I could see it in the way he dropped his napkin on the floor and slid his unfinished burger into the trash bin.

When we got to my little house, he reached behind him and practically punched me in the stomach to push me off. I said, in my loud ticket-taker voice, "Thank you," hell-bent on pretending I hadn't ruined everything. He answered with silence and peeled out.

That night, while eating strawberry ice cream with gummy bears, a combination so sweet it hurt my entire face, I made a mental list of everything I was guilty about: I was guilty of gluttony and of coveting. Of thinking Sarah Braithwaite was dumpy and of ridiculing her for her fat ass. Of believing Jeremiah didn't deserve her. Of fearing I didn't deserve Jeremiah, which left me even guiltier, and bitter—I didn't like being at the bottom of the dog pile. I imagined doing something stupid, like telling Sarah I was in love with her boyfriend so she'd better watch out.

I went to bed and had a fit of sobbing, the kind where I felt sick in my heart, which filled the room as if trying to escape. Then it shrank to the size of an egg, translucent and breakable, in the aching hollow of my chest. I had the sudden, powerful desire to have a baby with Jeremiah, a baby who would belong to me, who I would love forever, who would take away the killing feeling of being so alone. It was absurd, and pitiable, and about as plausible as my threatening Sarah. For several minutes, however, the idea of that new, unblemished soul blotted out my guilt completely.

The next morning, I was sure that I had failed Jeremiah—he had done everything in his power to seduce me, and although he succeeded, I never gave him the affirmation he was after. I had acted like just another sister, after all (if, in fact, he had any sisters): I had told him how funny he was but not how handsome, how lucky, perhaps, but not how loved. As I scooped my heart out at the Glacier, smiling a lot and seeing my customers through a scrim of pain—this poor thing had truly horrifying acne, that one would surely be broken by love—I told myself a new lie. If Jeremiah walked in that door, I would let my words rush out with longing, with enthusiasm. I would tell him exactly what I felt for him in the various damaged but eager parts of my body. If he walked in, if he walked in...

In December, I graduated then quit my job at the theater to devote myself entirely to ice cream. Sarah worked the closing shifts, and I requested days. If he walked in, I wanted to be there.

It was spring before I stopped wearing my hope like a bright yellow ribbon, tangy-sweet, in the hair I brushed religiously, every night, to shining.

LIFE OF A HYDRA

MARINA WAS just hitting her stride on the treadmill, reaching that place where breathing and heart rate synchronize, where corpus and machine become allies, when she felt the first twinges of nausea. Had last night's Greek salad contained bad lettuce? It really got under her skin, the thought of a herd of Holsteins contaminating her greens, the non-green-eating farmer who hadn't trained his workers to properly cleanse their harvest. She pushed her legs harder, forcing through the mounting discomfort, and sipped sweet vitamin water. She had worked countless late nights since the start of the new year, had meticulously planned for this tri-weekly window of gym time, and goddammit if she was going to give over to some trick her body was playing. She concentrated on keeping her left foot from pronating, its tendency to twist sideways that upset her stride and twice had led to a pulled tendon. Then her face began to itch.

More accurately it resumed its itch, the irritation that was her latest obsession's sidekick, not unlike the teacup poodle that had persisted in leaving tiny turds in her purse, or those pearlescent silk underwear that both pinched and rode up. Everything bit back, she knew, rivulets of sweat beginning to snake down her cheeks, the itch becoming unbearable. She tried to focus on one of Club Olympia's myriad television screens, a morning show that trotted out tarted-up, prepubescent girls who then received makeovers, but all she wanted to do was rend her flesh until one pain canceled out the other. She slowed to a stop, grabbed a gym-issue towel, and mimed a delicate patting motion as she half-seriously fantasized about how good it would feel to get power-washed like an off-road vehicle.

In the locker room, she slammed the door of a bathroom stall and sat down hard, squeezed her eyes against the astringent odor of urine mixed with chlorinated pool water. Momentarily, she knew, hordes of children would emerge from swim class. She had to do this now before she got boxed in, held captive by their shivering bodies, their hair detangling, and the never-ending, serpentine line-up to put suit after suit into the water-shedding spinner with its maddening drone. In one fierce motion, she threw the towel over her face and began to scrub, almost letting go moans of pleasure as she launched her unrestrained attack upon the thing that was gnawing at her skin. Five minutes passed before she could bring herself to stop and let the cloth fall from her face. She massaged her wrenched and sore fingers, her mind replaying the sound she had just heard—a curious *thump.*

Blood pressure rising, Marina knew she was not all right. The itch might be in remission, but the towel now felt surprisingly heavy, while her face felt, well, lighter, sensitive to the faintest movements of the air, and tender, in an open-wound sort of way. Closing her eyes, she cautiously extended a finger to the bridge of her nose. Instead of velvety epidermis, smooth and warm and pliable, she found herself reaching into the very moist interior of her septum, into the raw architecture of bone and cartilage. Her entire body felt enormously weighted against the toilet seat, all gravity focused in her buttocks and thighs as she forced her eyes open. She stared and stared down, thought she might scream, clamped her hand over a mouth that no longer featured a pair of pillowy lips but was instead a gaping maw. Then the gagging began, her earlier nausea competing with this new revulsion, until fear froze her innards, barely held her together, her brain throbbing futilely in its skullcage. It was sheer good luck that, despite the impending heat of the day, she had grabbed a long-sleeved shirt and wrapped it around her waist to deflect from her less-than-exuberant areas. She would rip this into strips, somehow—she could use the serrated edge of the toilet paper dispenser—and use these to, to—she could barely tell herself—*tie on her face*. She didn't want to look down at it, her face—that had separated itself from her body and lay, with nose, lips, and ears still attached, upon her lap.

Her newest preoccupation had to be the culprit: for the magazine, she was trying out various high-end skincare brands, each labeled in antiseptic blue and white, or juicy neon orange, or mature glowing gold, all with promises of cosmetic renovation, all containing FDA-approved amounts of acids, enzymes, stem cells, and who-knew-what. Well, all not yet approved. Three times a day, as recommended, she massaged the stuff into her skin, counting from A to Z, although all of it, whether curdling in her cupped hands, fizzing on her fingertips, or oozing out of amber droppers, looked repulsive, like the coagulant causatum of liposuction.

Immediately after each round, her skin turned translucent, approximating the invisi-pored dewiness of that rare, enviable subspecies of teenager who possessed a preternaturally radiant stretch across their occipitofrontalis and around their orbicularis oris, the ones with the most edible-looking fat pads beneath their cheekbones. On the day following the completion of each trial, however, little red bumps appeared along the edge of her jaw, next to her ears and above her hairline. These were easily covered by makeup until, within another day or two, the bumps multiplied, grew, and began to prickle as if something were crawling inside. She tried but was unable to ignore the scales of dead derma that began to form around her eyes, nose, and mouth, accompanied by an untenable tautness at the corners of same. The muscular stress of this downward-pulling tension further aggravated her unhappy situation. By evening of the fourth day, she had to admit there was no way the bloodied patches on her cheeks, nose, chin, and forehead could be mistaken for the blush of health. Wrecked and miserable, she saw no option but to restore herself with the next treatment kit.

She had earned the right to blame and complain. She could already look back on the years she had been in demand, the day she was crowned managing editor of *TRÉS PHYSIQUE!* when it was still in print. Now that they were completely online, she increasingly relied upon Breel, the girl's unimpeachable research into synergistic futurewear, overnight exercise and water-based diets. Marina plugged these tidbits into her own old features and kept the byline, but even she could see how the articles simpered. For ages there had been no romantic interest worth dissecting over lunch—she wasn't about to discuss her habit of sexting exes after-hours. Most of her current fantasies starred Goji, the too-young intern, and if "hanging out" at Game Galleria was the only means to that end, she was better off alone at home, downing pitchers of Aqua Velva cocktails until she passed out. Breel was the final insult, always at her elbow, chattering ingenuously, processing information at lightning speed. The twenty-two-year-old possessed a more formidable word-stock, business chic and unwavering self-esteem than Marina had ever thought to ask from herself, let alone feel beholden to in an assistant. Just give me better, brighter skin, she had asked the collection of sea-green-tinted vessels.

She drove the speed limit and signaled long before changing lanes, sunglasses holding her brow in place. From her nose down, she wore the teal gym towel like a veil and had managed to tie pieces of the cotton shirt across her upper lip and chin. She was grateful for her tinted windows but frustrated that she had to leave them one-third open because she hadn't fixed the air-conditioning. It was June and already quite hot; organic matter putrefied in such heat.

Her first call was to the magazine. Breel, although concerned, seemed enthused to be put in charge while her boss took a sudden leave of absence. Marina tried to ask casually for the number of the plastic surgeon who, on occasion, took Breel out for a drink, the doctor who had made masterpieces of many of Breel's friends' noses and thighs. Lean, Nordicly nostrilled Breel was in no need of any such realignment.

"Oh, Mar!" Breel drew in her breath hesitantly, and Marina could just imagine what superb office gossip the girl thought she was getting, "Is this about that tummy tuck?" Next, Marina contacted the office of Dr. Dennis Herkle, scalpel-wielding aesthete supreme. Talk might be all over the magazine in a matter of hours, but not before she was prepped and on the table in the doctor's private operating room.

Herkle was barely five feet tall and as polished as a fine walking stick. His forearms bulged beneath rolled-up sleeves that exposed a platinum watchband dwarfed by a matching, Egyptian-style cuff. As he examined Marina's face, which she handed to him with repugnance, he ventured a smile, one eyetooth winking brightly from behind a half-raised curtain of healthy, pink lip.

"We'll have to use it, I'm afraid—not enough rear end on you to make a proper frenulum, let alone nose and ears,"—she decided this was intended as a compliment—"but essentially it'll be like starting from scratch," he said. "So, which archetype most incites your envy?"

Marina took a moment to digest this information then went for broke. "I could work with a Bambi Klaus nose, cheekbones like Barucha Turkington's, a Sabrina Crawfish mouth…"

"I'll do my best," Dr. H. promised, introducing the anesthesiologist. The three of them counted backward, and just before Marina's abrupt disappearance into the dead time that Herkle called "the laying on of hands," she heard her doctor clap his surgical gloves together and utter a soft, happy sigh.

She awoke without pain, her first thought for her job—would she still have one? Then when she closed her eyes, and again with them open, she was inundated with visions. She saw cutting-edge photo stories with irresistible, interactive layouts, a total revamping of the magazine—she grasped the bottle of pills Herkle placed into her hand, let herself be helped into a limousine and thereafter up some stairs, into an apartment that looked like hers, only it could use some redecorating—she had several schemes in mind—and slept for a week, dreaming vividly, in color, with panache.

Herkle's personal driver returned her to the doctor's office, and her bandages were removed. She didn't know herself. Herkle smiled triumphantly, patted her knee, and pointed out his patented cauterizing technique, which left no visible scarring. They took their time, admiring her newborn face in a perfectly round mirror.

She was Marina again, both less and more so. Each of her features had been slightly altered, and now, for the first time since childhood, they conspired toward integration. Whereas before, her close-set orbs magnified a downturned nose, which further cast its shadow upon the corners of a smallish, negative-seeming mouth, now the eyes, newly captivating, nudged one's attention to the outward sweep of the cheekbones, which encouraged nothing less than enthrallment with sweetly disposed lips, not to be outdone by neat little ears that naturally accentuated a beguiling tilt of nose, provoking pure admiration for the lusty, intelligent arc of forehead. Together, sculptor and muse gleamed each other.

"Please," Herkle finally broke the spell, "do me a favor."

"Name it, Dr. Hero," Marina practically sang, trying out a low-pitched, raspy enunciation. She had several inspirations for different hair, makeup, and clothing; she felt she should be driving a more streamlined vehicle, one of those electric supercars. She must add variety to her diet by way of exotic fruits and vegetables and resume taking vitamin supplements. Tomorrow she would speak with the manager of Club Olympia, which was badly in need of an equipment upgrade. This recovery room could use some throw pillows, too, and as for the last mob that had run for government office, well, it was no wonder—

"Assure me you will incinerate those skin creams," Dr. H. beamed. He handed her a small package of syringes and instructed her to use these instead, just at the hair- and jawline, to help speed up the healing. "These incorporate your own nervous fluids—your own moxie, so to speak—so they should not cause irritation. Use them and you will spring forth stronger."

"Deal," Marina smiled generously in return, giving herself goosebumps, then charged Herkle's entire, exorbitant fee to her Platinum card.

It was mostly quick and dirty after that. Every day she looked and felt better, until within a couple of weeks she was back at her desk. Breel had left this in impeccable order prior to taking vacation days at her family's farm in Vermont. Marina ignored Breel's compilation of energy drink data and prophetic insights into the benefits of plyometrics, along with the pile of employee-penned haikus incorporating synonyms for "abdomen," and instead called an all-staff meeting.

She paced the conference room like a coal-and-oil man eyeing federally protected wilderness. "*TRÉS PHYSIQUE!* must resemble athletic apparel crafted by the gods—easy to slip into but technologically performative, lightweight and layered with innovative features, bioluminescent, with wings. Onward!" She immediately drafted two articles, one newsworthy and the other pseudo-pastiche, based on theories she had read in this week's motivational best seller. She answered five hundred e-mails and then went to the gym. Newly worked-out, with a flood of chemicals lighting up her synaptic command center, she returned to the office and spotted her intern, who looked beyond fetching in black trousers about to slide off his narrow hips and an undershirt imprinted with crustaceans.

"Goji, I have a design project made just for you. But first, the article on no-stink synthetics—workout clothes dipped in that antibacterial substance found in crab shells? All yours. And dinner tonight to discuss your—er, the—finer points. Kay?" She felt ebulliently juvenile. Several hours later, she had him intoxicated and agreeable, at home and in her bed. Months of stagnant frustrations were emancipated, re-roped, teased out and strung from the literal rafters. She couldn't say what to call it except that expectations were met and then exceeded. Oh, Goji, you mad little squid. They slept into the next day, and he called in sick; she came in late but with a whole slew of brainchildren.

Each new day was a whirl, a gag, a breeze. Marina felt like a character out of a movie from the 1930s—musical themes accompanied her, and she bought a lot of yellow, with polka dots. Many popular advertising slogans that Marina had heard throughout her life, that had become erased aural wallpaper, now resonated in vibrant, pulsating relief: Just do it, because you're worth it, think different, the happiest place on earth. She *was* lovin' it, all of it, feeling her "real beauty," writing articles about armpits if they would sell her magazine. She could wear big hats to the office and midriff-revealing t-shirts to her workouts. She could breathe loudly and eat loudly and spend money recklessly; she could snort while laughing in public. So this was what other fortysomething women were talking about, arriving at their transcendent self-realizations—Marina felt as if she had been given a get-out-of-jail-free card, a five-pound tin of Danish butter cookies, and a loving, indulgent pat on the bottom.

Breel came back to work on Monday tan, fit, and with dark circles under her eyes. Her family's property included a small lake, and she talked about how she went swimming every morning, played chicken with her three older brothers and their friends. Marina overheard her telling Goji how the water turned golden in the afternoon sun, how they had fallen about on the grass and eaten ice cream in their wet bathing suits, each of them with their own pint. It was hard to explain why the simple sounds of Breel, the natural look of her, caused Marina such doubt, such pure spitting meanness. Faced with Breel's consistent and easy confidence, Marina felt her clarity shrink and her brain fill with fog until she was encased in it. Breel was a matter-of-fact force of nature, was resplendent and free, always had been and always would be, independent of her boss's consent or desire.

At her ergonomic standing desk, Marina steadied her breathing and considered how best to do what must be done. Goji and Breel had begun talking in whispers, and Marina didn't hear the rest: how the family had moved Breel's mother's bed into the guesthouse, how a hospice nurse had been called to administer morphine. She did see their embrace, the tender way Goji squeezed Breel's shoulder and seemed to linger before letting go. When Marina called her over, Breel quickly made her way through the corridor of cubicles until she stood in front of her boss's engraved stone nameplate, the simple but bold lettering, *M. Serpiente.* Breel opened her mouth to speak, and her eyes began to water.

Marina wanted to be kind. After she spoke, she felt bewildered but ignored the feeling. Instead, she switched her attention to other notions, champagne, oysters, and Goji chief among them. How pleasing that her rewired self had all the setting options of a spanking-new computer game.

What she said was, "Breel, dear, nothing personal, but we're letting you go. If you'd like, you don't have to stay the day."

Before filling her undeniably mod camera-style bag with her personal items and exiting the building for the last time, Breel asked, in the small, tentative voice of a child, "You okay, Mar? Your cheek is kind of…drooping."

Marina went directly to the gym; the exchange with Breel had been enervating. Only now, catching a glimpse of herself in the locker-room mirror, she could swear her face looked lopsided. Breathing faster, she turned away then back again, hoping to correct a trick of the light, and saw what Breel must have seen: a woman whose face was a soft, pink polyp, faintly throbbing, whose ear and eye and nose seemed to be melting. What had Herkle done? What was in those injectables? She tasted bile.

Light-headed, but now doubly determined to complete her workout, she applied powder without looking into any more mirrors and stalked back to the treadmill. She began to run—away from Breel and Goji in matching Converse All Stars, from Herkle's glossy Gucci slippers, from her own barnacled appendages, bungeed into plant-sourced, vegan leather trainers. She ran, faster and harder so that the thump, thump of her feet hitting the deck rattled up her legs and burned through her core. She ran until her head cleared and she could see herself at home, opening the cabinet beneath the bathroom sink to reveal a sizeable cache of colorful bottles. She had gathered these as insurance, against a product recall that hadn't happened. Now she saw herself placing the plug in the tub and beginning something new. She would pour herself a lake of product, of rejuvenation, of game plans and master plans and winning solutions, of pure, clean, eternal, unborn skin, a lake in which to immerse herself and seal the wound, bury the immortal head.

THE MONEY GAME

BISHOP AND DEIDRE and I eat at a cafeteria, a place where the food looks good up close under bright lights, laid in rows on slanted aluminum shelves, but where it all tastes like salt and Crisco, where we feel vaguely sympathetic toward the servers tottering on greasy, unsafe floors under the scowls of their thick-necked bosses, but where we also feel at home. We sit under a fake tree below a pretend balcony and eat selectively from melamine plates: the cream cheese frosting off a hunk of bitter red cake, the sweet potatoes beneath their cloying crust, none of the brined turkey but most of the dressing and canned cranberry jelly. Across from us, a boy of maybe two is teaching himself to laugh. When the adults around him wrench their faces into painful-looking contortions, he, too, poofs his cheeks maniacally and bares his gums. When the adults bray and snort, the child screeches and caws in closely observed imitation.

Dee rolls her eyes—*in ten years, is this how you want to be spending your Saturday nights?*—and smears a bite of cake into Bish's new jeans, massages it into the fabric that pulls tight across his slim thigh.

When Bish pushes her hand away, she finally gets to the point and invites us to join the Game.

"We could buy a house," Bishop huffs through a huge cloud of crystal. "Something in San Anselmo, something small but ours." I want to inhale as deeply, always want to occupy the same space as Bish, but my throat and lungs burn. I settle for holding my breath as long as I can, count down the minutes with lips pressed and eyes closed, blood pumping wildly. When I open my mouth, my eyes, my head springs free before bouncing back to Bish. Deirdre says we need the Game.

"You need the money," she says, our sweetest Dee.

"Thirty-two thousand dollars!" I envision a pathway through trees to a pale-yellow door, hardwood floors and window after window, letting in the sun.

Dee says capitalists come in all flavors. Do we want to be unhappy or happy hippies?

Bishop says to himself, "Shit. Shit."

Dee and I share a look. Who knows what he's thinking.

She says we need a healing. "At the Hermeticon Temple," she prescribes, eyes full of green light. She might play again.

At the Muir Psychic Academy, we sit in a circle and work with intuitive teachers who see into our thoughts, who charge a few hundred dollars for an eight-week course during which we build an interdimensional construct of trust. We learn how to enter into conscious agreements with healing masters in the metaphysical sphere; my healer resembles a Hakuna Matata version of Tarzan. One of our most compassionate MPA instructors, Peat, says the cause of my crying jags is too much male energy residing in my female body. This makes sense since it is men I mostly think about and give my autonomy to, and Peat tells me I can easily release the excess by blowing it up in a rose.

Psychic work, we begin to understand, is about directing our thoughts, a powerful form of energy, through a sequence of positive visualizations. We bring in gold suns and throw down grounding cords, and I feel better on the days I practice my psychic tools. I want to see auras and read "pictures," the images that form in the minds of sentient beings; we are assured these abilities will come in time when we enroll in Clairvoyance II.

Dee completes Clairvoyance II and goes on to earn her psychic bachelor's degree. After cashing out her Game winnings, sixteen thousand dollars, putting a measly two grand back into the Game must seem like a small investment in manifestation. Because she wants to circulate her winning energy, she invites us to lie on her bed so that she can cover our bodies with money. She tells us to roll in it, to visualize havingness. Some of the cash sticks together and scrapes my cheek, pokes me in the kidney. My t-shirt twists up uncomfortably.

"This is what abundance feels like," Dee says, grinning. She doesn't wear lipstick or mascara because she looks better without them, her skin almost transparent. After a few minutes, several hundred-dollar bills work their way under my bra and I can't stop thinking about how dirty money is, passing through so many hands. I look up at Dee and try to see her psychic pictures, but the only images that appear to me are bacteria magnets: kitchen sponges and men's beards. I have read that both contain fecal matter.

From my parents, I receive two thousand dollars as a birthday gift that seems destined for the Game, primed to turn into sixteen— if Dee can do it!—and Bish gets his from somewhere. I don't see him all the time lately even though we live together, but on Sunday we give our combined money to a Hermeticon acolyte who smiles with closed lips and welcomes us onto the first floor of her wealth-building structure.

Just six more, Deirdre says, six more people for us to rise, and then with everyone else adding their people, only two more levels—only four or five more spaces to fill—until we get to cash out. She explains that our Game looks like this:

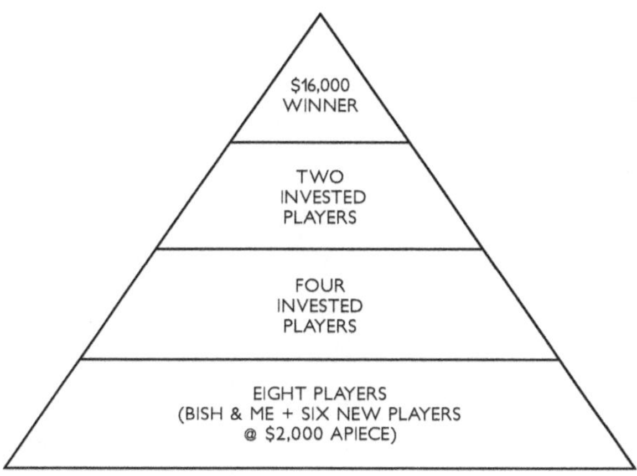

We could have simply done the math. We could have listened to the people who showed concern, who knew what they were talking about. We could have read more books about the occult, *The Master* by Colm Tóibín.

Deirdre: I have such news!

Bishop: Your medium has coughed up another diamond-encrusted hairball?

Deirdre: Ha-ha! I'm inviting you to join a marvelous game alongside the finest people.

Me: You're a love for thinking of us.

Bishop: Cost to join?

Deirdre: Exactly, you devil. (*Lowers voice*) I've played my two silver and turned them into four gold. !

Me: !

Bishop: Let's smoke on it. (*Inhales deeply, exhales*)

Deirdre: (*Turns down the lights, claps a copper bell between thumb and forefinger*) We shall visualize. Ooh, I feel breezes of good fortune!

Bishop: (*Inhales deeply, ignores rustling from beneath the table*)

Deirdre: (*Appreciatively*) A stiff and hottish breeze.

Me: !

Bishop: (*Speaks while holding smoke in his lungs*) Too jolly good to be true.

We meet regularly on Sundays to work the positivity around
our Game, but our wealth-building group is poorly attended. Bish
and I often show up sleepless, still high from the night before. There
should be nine of us, but it is Sunday, after all—church and family,
and people get sick, maybe. Everyone is nice in a hopeful, desperate
way, and the numbers never make sense to me, so I leave that part to
Bishop. Philosophy major, economics minor, Berkeley grad. Bish asks
around and discovers the Short Game, five hundred to play and only
four people needed to cash out with two thousand, a way to get back
his seed money. *Four more bodies* is how they say it. We're not sure why
Dee hasn't joined our group, but we assume she is in another, "giving
back" as she said she would, except we don't usually see her on Sundays,
not even once now that I think back on it.

I don't want to say too much about how it feels to smoke, but
imagine swallowing the world. You've been feeling raw lately, which
makes sense, and after smoking just once, life will become comfortable
again, a velvet nest realigned. When the drug enters your lungs, your
heart, your brain, you'll believe that more smoke will somehow increase
your equilibrium although this is, by definition, impossible. After
many hours, days, and weeks of smoke, anxiety will rent a room, then a
penthouse in your head, will invite its hardscrabble friends—paranoia,
morbidity, despair—to languish and put their tang on your furnishings,
to consume your emergency rations. You'll begin to be erased. This is
not entirely painful although pain is involved: you are that much closer
to an unpleasant death. What will save you, after everything you care
about has been broken, is sheer dumb luck, your predisposition to
become easily bored—all obsessions become boring, eventually. Except
maybe not for Bish.

Why Bishop? Because I know what to make of him even if the
straight world doesn't. His narrow English suits, his prominent French
nostrils. His fierce, combative intelligence. How he anticipates high-
stakes negotiations, dictates favorable terms, cries and laughs like a two-

year-old. The way he writes indescribably moving, terrible poetry, delays us for hours by misplacing his keys and wallet, blames the supernatural realm for their unnerving reappearance. How he loves his furry creatures to death: his rat, his ferret, his chinchilla, overfeeds them one week, forgets to fill their water containers the next, lets their hair tangle and their cages sit outside in the burning sun, vulnerable to poisonous insects. He is the sincerest borderline personality I have ever met.

Am I trying to heal Bish by sharing his drugs?

After a couple of weeks, we experience lateral movement. Finally! Lucy, who knows Bishop through the New School where they accumulate loans in exchange for graduate degrees, invests one month's rent in our Game. We three will manifest together! This is not like pushing Ginsu or SuperVitamins because the Game has no gimmick, it is pure actualization.

I see Lucy is crushing on Bish the same way I did, hard out of the gate. She has a fresh scar on her face from a car accident, and when she talks to Bishop, she unconsciously pinches her upper lip and rubs off the concealing make-up. The thin white line that stretches across her philtrum is now exposed. I see she will do anything he asks.

Deirdre reminds us that getting a psychic healing is a good way to protect our Game investment, to clear lingering obstacles from our energetic paths. Bish says one significant form of negative energy is holding on too tightly—to anything, really, but when it comes to money especially, we must respect the idea of flow. Letting go of money, a form of tithing, triggers energetic movement that will allow us to get more of what we really need. We have taken the first step by handing over our combined four thousand dollars, and now we must clear out the old beliefs, implanted by our parents and assorted ancestors, in order for the flow to give back to us. This really does make as much sense as the male/female energetic predicament explained to me by Peat in our Psychic I course. I never feel as clever as when I agree with Bishop.

At the Hermeticon Temple, the wait for our healings feels claustrophobic and busy with workers eyeballing us in that impersonal way that means our pictures are being read. Bishop and I know we're not supposed to be intoxicated, for exacting rules are posted in the Hermeticon literature, but we arrive high anyway. Maybe this is why Jeff, the temple elder, comes into the room and scans us. Maybe this is why Jeff then selects a certain Hermeticon healer to work on us—to teach us a lesson. Or maybe we are being paranoid and our healer is, in fact, an unusually skilled adept who needs only sixty seconds to scour our chakras. Maybe she can see that we will immediately plug them back up.

I go first, into a small, plain room where I have been instructed to climb upon a table while remaining fully clothed. The table is hard, the kind we ate our elementary school lunches on, and I lie there for what feels like a long time before the healer jerks in with a bad-day attitude. She is humerus-and-clavicle thin, dressed in black with black lipstick and purple-black hair. Her hands, as they hover next to my body, reek of cigarette smoke. I suddenly see pictures of brown toothbrushes and toilet brushes and then, in the extreme, of Bosch-like, tormented creatures leaking thick, yellowish-black smoke and fluids from their eyes and ears and so on. I can't say it feels good to allow these images into the room, so I try to blow roses and send the pictures down my grounding cord, into the molten center of the Earth that can transmogrify all energy. The healing is over in less time than I spent waiting on the table, and I return to the lobby just as Bish's name is called. Minutes later, he too has been healed by the same person.

"What a rip," he says. But now that we are outside, I see that he is floating several inches above the sidewalk.

I contrast this healing with the Reiki treatment I receive days later at a woodsy natural springs retreat in NorCal where Bish and I get methed out of our minds. Between rounds of limb-numbing sex followed by my inability to walk outside of our cabin, we discuss our Hermeticon healer. I try to feel empathy for her as a whole person: she was once an adorable infant, a dimple-kneed toddler, a saucy six-year-old, a precocious preteen, a valedictorian. I understand that she is us, but I keep losing the thread, the thing that I am moving toward or in retreat from: if I am in love with Bishop—and never have I fallen this deeply—then why do I feel so rotten?

I am finally able to leave our room by scheduling the Reiki. The fee for this, plus our days at the retreat, the food and drink we order in, and the movies we rent, all go on my credit card, which I will pay off when we cash out of the Game. In a tent warmed by the adjacent hot springs, I collapse on a yoga table and am covered with a cool, white cloth. As soon as the Reiki therapist lays hands on me, I sob. She does something with my pain, turns it into butterflies that become dissolving holograms, instructs each of my major organs to release the toxic burden it carries, gives me permission to stop trying with Bish. Tarzan, my personal psychic healer, stands in the corner of the tent with his furry arms crossed, nodding. He has a long cat's tail whose slinky susurration calms me. What the Reiki master and Tarzan don't see is that leaving Bishop will always feel like him leaving me.

Back at home, with so much volatile, addictive sex and how Bish pulls on my attention, convinces me that meat is murder, that gender is mutable, that his crystal visions reveal truth—I don't see it coming when he says he slept with Deirdre all last year. When I think of them spending so many random hours in her doll-sized flat, her human birdhouse surrounded by trees, I can't breathe.

The one time I climb her narrow, forever stairs and duck inside, I gasp, dizzied by the beauty and strangeness of her view: how the swirl inside her irises is the storm that spins outside her windows. How everything about her beguiles.

I can play this way, too. I use the Game as an excuse to talk to Real Foods Jeremy beyond our "amazing peaches" exchanges and succeed in asking him to dinner. He is so good-looking that waiting for him to call makes my stomach hurt with the terror of rejection and potentially thwarted lust. I speak carefully about our meeting because I don't want to share him with Bishop, certainly not with Deirdre.

When Jeremy shows up hours late, we both order the overly rich pumpkin ravioli at the same place I go whenever I have dinner without Bishop. Over coffee, Jeremy says no to the Game, very kindly and definitively. Afterward, we have sex in the house he shares with a biker who keeps a fifteen-foot baby python, but somehow I miss it, the sex. I remember touching Jeremy's face for a long time, and when we finally take off our clothes, I leave my body.

After receiving Jeremy's no, and because with only Lucy our Game will stall, I feel deflated.

"Don't forget," Deirdre keeps saying, "everyone needs at least two bodies apiece. That's when you'll split." According to Deirdre, for both Bish and me to move up a level, to move closer to pay-out, our single Game will have to look like this:

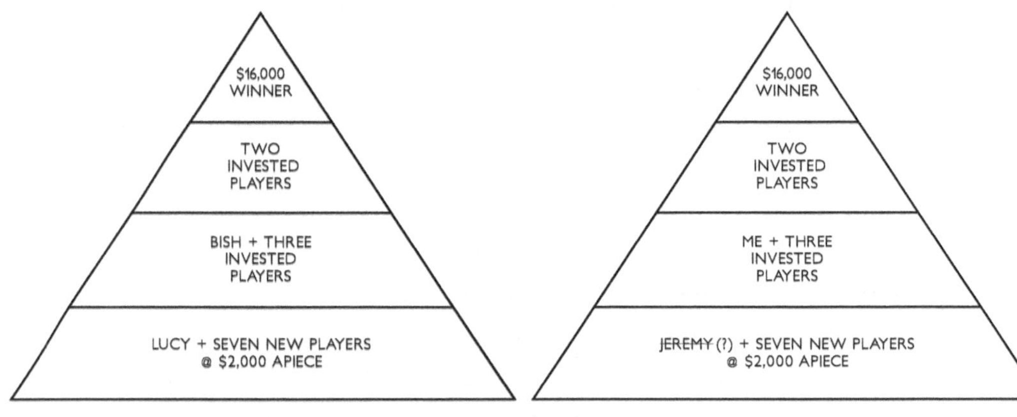

We are flummoxed. We will no longer be in the same Game? Lucy will have to find an additional seven players? Our community will be tapped out quickly if everyone is looking for bodies—maybe it is already tapped out. I try not to look at the schemata too closely.

Bish invites Deirdre over to smoke, to clear the negative energy, and the three of us have sex, which is scary at first, imagining how she and I look to Bishop when he stops to watch us, then less so, then exhausting. Afterward, we rent a hot tub, and Deirdre calls up the person she is dating, who joins us, and who, after a while, turns questioning eyes on each of us, but I can't do anything extra. I am tapped out.

Two weeks sober, I go by myself to a lecture by a famous clairvoyant. I sit in the back of the auditorium and study this magic man intently, challenge myself to identify the colors of his light-body. I feel his magnetism, his oceans of steady electricity, but his words bypass my ears, my brain, and the only thing I can see is my need to see something. As the audience shuffles out, he maneuvers through the crowd and pops up next to me, turns his probing gaze on my third eye.

"Don't you love looking for auras?" he smiles, and I am struck by how easy I must be to read. How disheartening that I have not learned to pull in my energy and melt, unnoticed, into the background, that I will probably never see anybody's rings of emanation.

When Bishop—at last—has his moment of insight and figures out the numbers, he stands up so quickly that his chair flips over and bounces across the floor. We are at a Sunday morning Game meeting, just us and one other wealth-building group member, and Bish wails, furious at himself, bereft with disappointment, confirming what we already know. His outburst feels good to me, freeing; something needed to tear through the sedate dispirit that has fallen over our group like a slowly tightening net. He calls Lucy to break the news. Although he promises to pay her back, I worry about how he's going to get the money. Lucy doesn't hang out with us after that.

Before and after the Game: before, the world feels too big, too full of fantastical possibilities, of never-ending options. After, the world becomes ridiculously small for a while. Not small the way it is for certain children who dig through piles of garbage to search for anything to sell besides themselves, who carry cast-off bottles of chemical products with enough scum at the bottom to mix with their spit, who inhale this mixture, who finally swallow poison. Small, instead, with self-pity and disgust.

It takes a long time for me to heal, for the smoke-desire to go away. I don't remain friends with Deirdre, but I hear that she gets married and has babies. Bishop goes to rehab, just once as far as I know, and we lose touch after that. After more transcendental work, I decide that psychics and gurus are invasive species—I don't want to read people's minds. I continue to feel this way even after I am much older and have become the kind of person who treats my body like a temple, who is genuinely concerned about the fate of *Homo sapiens,* who tries to convince much younger people that I know what I am talking about.

ACKNOWLEDGMENTS

An earlier version of "Babylove" appeared in *The Ilanot Review*.

I'd like to thank Mona Houghton and Kevin Cantwell, who made this book a reality; my San Diego writing group, especially Lisa Shapiro and Deborah Reed, who read the earliest drafts of many of these stories; and Mona Ray Scully, Kevin Scully, Blair Davis, Marty Davis, and Diane Mitchell, whose friendship saw me through it all.

TAMAR PERLA CANTWELL'S fiction has appeared in journals and anthologies including *The Ilanot Review, The North American Review, Ascent, Monologues from the Road,* ed. Lavonne Mueller, and *Secrets,* ed. Linny Stovall. Her nonfiction essay, "Transmissions and Transgressions of the Holy," was a finalist in the New Letters Literary Awards. Tamar was a writer-in-residence at the Djerassi Resident Artists Program in Woodside, California. She received her BA in English from the University of California, Berkeley, where she was lucky to take a poetry class with Ishmael Reed; she received her MA in creative writing at San Francisco State University, where she studied with Molly Giles. Tamar taught composition for ten years in San Diego, California, and currently, she is the assistant director of the Academic Resource Center at Mercer University in Macon, Georgia.

LOS ANGELES

All WHAT BOOKS feature cover art by Los Angeles painter, printmaker, muralist, and theater and performance artist GRONK. A founding member of ASCO, Gronk collaborates with the LA and Santa Fe Operas and the Kronos Quartet. His work is found in the Corcoran, Smithsonian, LACMA, and Riverside Art Museum's Cheech Marin collection.

As a small, independent press, we urge our readers to support independent booksellers. This is easily done on our website by purchasing our books from Bookshop.org.

WHATBOOKSPRESS.COM

2023

God in Her Ruffled Dress
LISA B (LISA BERNSTEIN)
POEMS

Figures of Wood
MARÍA PÉREZ-TALAVERA
TRANSLATED BY PAUL FILEV
NOVEL

A Plea for Secular Gods: Elegies
BRYAN D. PRICE
POEMS

Nightfall Marginalia
SARAH MACLAY
POEMS

Romance World
TAMAR PERLA CANTWELL
STORIES

2022

No One Dies in Palmyra Ohio
HENRY ELIZABETH CHRISTOPHER
NOVEL

Us Clumsy Gods
ASH GOOD
POEMS

Skeletal Lights From Afar
FORREST ROTH
FLASH FICTION/PROSE POEMS

That Blue Trickster Time
AMY UYEMATSU
POEMS

2021

Pyre
MAUREEN ALSOP
POEMS

What Falls Away Is Always
KATHARINE HAAKE &
GAIL WRONSKY, EDITORS
ESSAYS

*The Eight Mile
Suspended Carnival*
REBECCA KUDER
NOVEL

Game
M.L. WILLIAMS
POEMS

2020

No, Don't
ELENA KARINA BYRNE
POEMS

One Strange Country
STELLA HAYES
POEMS

*Remembering Dismembrance:
A Critical Compendium*
DANIEL TAKESHI KRAUSE
NOVEL

Keeping Tahoe Blue
ANDREW TONKAVICH
STORIES

2019

Time Crunch
CATHY COLMAN
POEMS

Whole Night Through
L.I. HENLEY
POEMS

Echo Under Story
KATHERINE SILVER
NOVEL

Decoding Sparrows
MARIANO ZARO
POEMS

W H A T
BOOKS
PRESS

LOS ANGELES